Rim the Caprock

Rim of the Caprock

NOEL M. LOOMIS

Sagebrush
Large Print Westerns

Library of Congress Cataloging-in-Publication Data

Library of Congress CIP Data was not provided in time for publication. Please call (800) 818-7574 or (603) 772-1175 in the U.S. or Canada and we will fax or mail it to you.

Cataloguing in Publication Data is available from the British Library and the National Library of Australia.

Sagebrush Large Print Westerns are published in the United States and Canada by Thomas T. Beeler, Publisher, PO Box 659, Hampton Falls, New Hampshire 03844-0659. ISBN 1-57490-273-3

Published in the United Kingdom, Eire, and the Republic of South Africa by Isis Publishing Ltd., 7 Centremead, Osney Mead, Oxford OX2 0ES England. ISBN 0-7531-6257-1

Published in Australia and New Zealand by Bolinda Publishing Pty. Ltd., 17 Mohr Street, 3043, Tullamarine, Victoria, Australia. ISBN 1-74030-010-6

Manufactured by Sheridan Books in Chelsea, Michigan.

TO THE MEN AND WOMEN OF THE LLANO ESTACADO

THEY WERE OF MANY OCCUPATIONS AND OF DIVERSE nationalities, but they conquered a land that adventuring pioneers had avoided for fifty years, a land rigorous with wind and drought, of which Charlie Goodnight said it produced better cattle, so why shouldn't it produce better men? Let this dedication include the Indians—Cheyennes, Kiowas, and especially the Comanches who had conquered the Staked Plains long before the white man came, and who made their final tragic stand on America's last frontier—the High Plains that had mothered them for generations.

Rim the Caprock

CHAPTER 1

THE HEAVY BOOM OF A FIFTY-CALIBER SHARPS RIFLE drifted down from the Caprock and brought an abrupt cessation of movement to the eight tall-hatted, leather-faced ranchmen waiting at the bottom of the Yellowhouse canyon.

They heard the shot and froze for an instant where they were hunkered down on their toes before a hitch rack along which their horses were standing. Then their heads turned in unison, eyes upward and to the southwest, and they scanned the Caprock eight hundred feet above them.

Newton, a lanky, long-mustached cowman from Louisiana, reached for his clumsy old .54 Navy pistol and said in a high, tense voice: "There's your signal! I knew they'd be on the warpath if they came. That's what you get for asking the Comanches to a conference."

Clay Hamilton had been whittling on a piece of fragrant cedar. He tossed the stick away, closed his big jackknife with a loud click, and rose to his feet. As did most of the others, he wore an ordinary colored shirt without a collar and open at the collar band; over the shirt he wore a woolly vest from an old brown suit, with its pockets handy for makings and matches. He had on heavy woollen trousers from the same suit, and wore the legs outside his boots. He was slightly built but appeared as tough as *bois d'arc*. His wide hatbrim was curled to a point in front and pulled low. Now, with head tilted back, he watched the Caprock with keen gray eyes.

1

"It was only one shot," he said with a nasal Missouri twang. "He was supposed to give us two when he saw the Indians—three if they come loaded for bear."

Tompkins, tall, lean, and thoughtful, pointed out: "He might have intended to fire again, but he's in trouble with the big gray."

Wilbarger, short, compact, and wearing the only black hat in the Yellowhouse valley, said in a distinct Southern drawl, "It isn't that I mind gettin' scalped so much—but I *would* like to see it comin'."

The man on the edge of the Caprock, at that distance no more than a tiny black silhouette against the West Texas sky, was trying to approach his horse, but the animal kept backing away. A small cloud of black-powder smoke, faint at that distance but plain against the clear sky, drifted south.

"That fool Shorty!" Dow Jones said with an explosive violence that betrayed his tension. "I *told* him to let that hammerhead soak a while before he forked him."

They all were on their feet now. "He'd a been all right," said Wilbarger, "if he hadn't of hung onto the bridle reins while he fired that buffalo cannon."

"He'll be all right anyhow," said Clay Hamilton in his strong Missouri twang. "He always ties the *mecate* around his waist. Shorty'd ruther be drug home than walk home."

Wilbarger announced suddenly, "He's pointing downcanyon."

They all turned downcanyon together and saw the motivation for Shorty's signal. Half an hour's easy ride down the Yellowhouse, where the canyon began to widen out, they could see a cloud of dust in the center of the valley, plain above the dull green splotch of a small marsh.

2

Hamilton let out a short breath of relief. "It's a pilgrim."

Newton turned to scan the Caprock opposite nervously. "I still think it was askin' for trouble to invite the Comanches down here."

"I thought," said Hamilton, "we'd better try to come to an agreement before we started killing them—or before they start killing us."

Wilbarger studied Newton, and nodded slightly as if in basic agreement with him. "It's no use gettin' het up about it. There'll be time for that when they show up." He spoke to Hamilton. "Where do you reckon that outfit's from?"

"They must have come up the Brazos from Fort Griffin—but where are they headed and what are they after?"

Tompkins said speculatively, "They can't get up on top of the Caprock anywhere around here—and that's the only place where there's any free grass left."

Dow Jones, squinting with his one good eye, said, "He's got no stock."

"Maybe he thinks he's in the Running Water canyon. There's a door to the Caprock up there that the comancheros use for their carts." He gave the word a Spanish pronunciation: co-man-chay´ros.

Doug Campbell spoke up in his burry voice, "Perhaps he has a good rope and a set of dotting irons, as Mr. Hamilton has so aptly put it."

There was embarrassed silence for a moment, for all of those present but the two Scotsmen, who were new in the Panhandle, knew that when Clay Hamilton spoke of those implements he was thinking of Gordon Gault.

"Do you reckon," Dow Jones asked quickly, "that could be one of them comancheros comin' up here?"

MacLeod, the second Scotsman, asked, "Are you speaking of Indians?"

Hamilton said, "No, the comancheros are men who trade with the Indians."

"You don't speak of them with approbation," Doug Campbell noted.

Tompkins, watching the distant outfit, said with distaste: "They're usually whites or Mexicans or halfbreeds. Mostly they come from New Mexico, but some come from the south around the Pecos and San Antonio, and some come up the Canadian River from Fort Smith. They've been at it since about 1780, and it's hard to stop."

"What's bad about it?" asked MacLeod.

"The comancheros are at the bottom of a lot of our Indian trouble. They pack stuff on burros or in carts or wagons and go to the meeting places up on the Plains— Mucha Que or Las Tecovas or along Las Lenguas just below the Caprock."

"At one time," Hamilton said, "they met here in this canyon."

"But—"

"They trade bread and cloth and trinkets for silver, turquoise, buffalo robes—anything as long as it's mostly cattle and horses," Clay said with a wry smile.

"And they encourage the Indians to steal the stock from us," Newton added bitterly.

"Surely the law—" MacLeod began.

"There's no law out here but what we make ourselves, Clay told him. "Indian Territory is wild; Kansas and Arkansas are too far away; and in the territories the federal government still looks on Texians as whipped rebels. That's why I figured the best thing was to talk to the Indians. Maybe we can get somewhere

4

that way."

"Speaking of Indians—" began Doug Campbell, but stopped short as two quick shots floated down from the Caprock.

The ranchmen turned together. Newton tried to say something but choked, for twelve elaborately feathered and ceremoniously beaded Indians of the northern Comanches—they called themselves Quahadi—had seemingly materialized in the bottom of the canyon and now were riding their stocky, close-coupled Plains mustangs down the trail on the other side of the creek.

Wilbarger looked at them warily. "They're smooth customers," he said. "A minute ago they were nowhere in sight. They got into this canyon right under Shorty's nose."

"They're on the warpath!" MacLeod said apprehensively. "They've come to lift our hair."

Clay reassured him. "No, the Plains Indians are horse Indians. They're the finest horsemen in the world, and when they're on a raid they don't carry any extra baggage. They strip down to moccasins and breechclout when they're out for business." He breathed a deep sigh of relief. "No, everything is all right," he said thankfully.

The Indians came on at a dignified walk. They crossed the Yellowhouse River, their horses splashing through the fetlock-deep water, and pulled up in the shade of a big twisted cottonwood tree halfway between the ranchers and the creek.

Clay Hamilton slid the jackknife into the pocket of his woolen pants and hitched up the pink elastic arm bands on his shirt sleeves. He stepped out, leading the way to the big cottonwood tree where the Indians waited. The ranchmen followed him, walking awkwardly and laboriously, in the way of men used to the saddle but unaccustomed to walking. They moved in unison, all big-hatted, all wearing vests, and today all wearing chaps, their one concession to formal dress—the only one possible for cowmen on that frontier. All but Hamilton were armed—against his wishes; all wore spurs which clinked in unison as they strode over the sun-baked ground, and the two-and-a-half-inch wheels of Wilbarger's Mexican spurs jangled musically as each foot came down, and the spur chains tinkled while the rowels scraped the earth and spun for an instant.

Clay looked the Indians over. They were a bright copper color, and most of them were young. Quanah Parker, the half-white Indian chief, had ridden a beautiful chestnut-and-white pinto that nuzzled him now in the back. Quanah himself showed little evidence of his mother's white blood; he was said to be under forty, though with his grim face and the deep wrinkles between his eyes he could have been much older.

The Indians all were short but well proportioned. Some wore copper bands on their left wrists for protection from their bowstrings, but today they all seemed to be unarmed. They had come in full ceremonial dress, with long, close-fitting buckskin leggings that reached to the hip. Some were naked above the waist; others wore painted buckskin vests. Some had feathers in their braided black hair, and Quanah Parker wore a beaded vest and a Sioux-type headdress with long trailing tails of eagle feathers.

The ranchmen reached the tree and stopped on the near side.

"Howdy," said Hamilton.

The chief grunted and nodded slowly. "You asked to talk with Quahadi. We have come."

6

"Glad you're here," said Clay.

Those around him seemed ill at ease, not knowing whether to stand or sit, but, perhaps due to the fact that the Comanches were standing, they elected to stand also—all but Dow Jones, who found a spot to sit on an exposed root of the cottonwood, and arranged his game leg carefully before him, with the sheepskin chap under it as a pad.

Quanah Parker showed no fear. He was grim and he seemed to have little expectation of good results from this meeting, but he waited for Clay Hamilton to speak.

"I sent word for you to come here," Hamilton said, "so we could talk things over. Down here in the Yellowhouse we're losing too much stock. At the last full moon your Indians took sixty head of cows and some horses." He shook his head slowly. "We can't stand losses like that. Some of the boys are in favor of calling on the Army, but some of the rest of us figured we ought to talk to you first."

"We have come," Quanah Parker said gravely, "without rifles, without arrows."

Clay nodded, pleased.

"You have promised no fighting," Quanah went on, then observed, "but your brothers have pistols and knives."

Clay's jaws tightened. He had been almost alone in his desire to meet the Indians to work out a peaceful settlement; the others had yielded, but when it came to leaving their arms at home he had been overruled. Now he said carefully: "The Comanches are as many as the wild mustangs. We are few, and my brothers do not know the customs of the Indians. But I know the Comanche keeps his word. My brothers will learn."

A flicker of satisfaction came and went in Quanah

Parker's eyes. He said, "The white man keeps his—when it suits him."

There was a little stirring among the ranchmen, but Quanah only eyed them sardonically. The warriors around him were impassive, but their black eyes saw every movement. "The white man wants grass," Quanah went on. "Always more grass for his cattle. He goes everywhere. Where he goes, he chases away the buffalo and destroys the Quahadi's hunting ground. He does not pay for the grass we have owned for many generations. He does not ask if we want to sell. He comes. The buffalo goes."

Hamilton said shrewdly, "The State of Texas gave us permission to come here. If your land is taken illegally, the state will settle with you."

"Very fine words," Quanah said bitterly. He fixed a piercing gaze on Clay. "For a hundred years," he said, "my people followed the war trail to the south as soon as summer's heat was over and the moon was full. Now there are many ranchers, many soldiers on the Pecos. White men offer a bounty on Comanche scalps. The old trail is closed to us." He went on steadily: "For a hundred years the Quahadi hunted game in the Wichita Mountains to the east. Now the soldiers at Fort Sill try to put him on a reservation, and many of my people have been killed." He raised a short, vigorous arm, and its fringed buckskin sleeve swept the country to the southeast. "For a hundred years before your people came to Texas," he said, "the Quahadi were in this country, fighting their enemies, riding with friends, killing the antelope and the buffalo for food, using the buffalo's hide for many things. But now the country east of the Caprock is forbidden. What is left?"

He raised his war-bonneted head and looked long at

the Caprock in the southwest. "There is left," he said in a low voice, "only the Llano Estacado, where the Quahadi have ruled for many years. There is little water up there, but the Quahadi have learned to find what little there is. There are no hills to break the north wind, but the Quahadi have learned to stand the cold."

He looked back at the ranchmen. He looked down the Yellowhouse, bounded on the southwest by the purple and brown of the shadowed Caprock, and on the opposite side by the same escarpment, which rose straight out of the ground, a rugged, forbidding barrier that showed red and yellow in the direct light of the sun. His gaze traveled the length of the valley, to the point where it seemed to drop away from the sky. Along the center of the valley, a dark green strip marked the course of the stream, but as the bottom rose on each side to meet the Caprock, the green faded, until at the very foot of the escarpment the grass grew only in sparse clumps mixed with mesquite bushes and occasional white spikes of bear grass. But everywhere, in the lush bottom and up the steep sides among the mesquite, the valley was dotted with grazing longhorns.

"You have taken the good land. You have come to the foot of the Llano," Quanah Parker said. "How long will you stay below the Plains? How long before you will be up there?"

Clay Hamilton drew a deep breath and looked away.

Quanah answered: "Only until you find a *puerta*—a pass for your wagons. Then what will be left for the Quahadi when your cattle swarm over the Plains?"

The ranchmen had stood uneasily under his tongue-lashing. Now Wilbarger drawled: "There won't be any cattle left when your Comanches get through stealing them. The way you fellows operate, it's out-and-out

9

thievery. We don't let a white man do that."

Quanah Parker turned to him. "You take from us our food, our shelter, our land. There is nothing for a young brave to do—no more fighting with the Navajos; the Navajos are on a reservation. No more fighting with the Wichitas; the Wichitas have been scattered by the soldiers. No more war parties to Durango, for the Pecos is closed to the Quahadi. Then come the comanchero traders—Mexicans, whites, half-breeds—many are your own people. They offer trinkets and whisky to my braves for horses and cattle. They know the Quahadi has never raised horses or cattle. The white man's cows are eating Quahadi grass. What is bad, then, if Quahadi take a few cows to trade with the comancheros?"

"We ain't responsible," Dow Jones said emphatically from his seat on the cottonwood root, "for what them white-trash comancheros do. If we had our way, we'd clean 'em out for good."

"You make me promise," Quanah Parker said to them all, "that cattle not go up on the Llano, I make you promise: no more stealing." He stood a little apart. He looked up at the Caprock, a man of dignity, of pride, and of courage, and with a sadness that dimmed his eyes. In a heavy voice he said finally, "Is last home of the Quahadi—up there."

There was silence for a moment. Then Wilbarger cleared his throat. Tompkins took from his vest pocket the flattened Minié ball which had been extracted from his back during the war, and which he carried for good luck. He tossed it up and down in his hand a couple of times. Dow Jones looked down at his sheepskin-chapped leg stretched out before him. Hamilton's mouth was tight.

"A promise wouldn't mean anything," Hamilton

admitted at last. "There will be others coming from the East, and I can't promise for them."

"If I make promise," said Quanah, "all my braves keep promise, or I bury them to the neck in anthill. Why you not make your brothers keep promise?"

Hamilton shook his head. "I am not a great, wise father," he said, "but I'll make you a deal: you leave my stock alone and I'll give you a beef every week for your people. Maybe some of the others will pitch in too."

"I'll give one beef a week," said Wilbarger.

Clay hitched up the belt of his chaps and looked at Quanah Parker. "There's something I'd like to ask you about," he said. "My daughter had a blue roan stallion that was her favorite riding horse. The Comanches took it three weeks ago. Can you get it back?"

Quanah Parker's eyelids dropped a fraction. He looked toward the big dobe ranch house beyond the hitch rack, where Madeline Hamilton was sitting on the front step. "In Quahadi country best horses are ridden by braves—but then Quahadi squaws not as beautiful as white squaw." He went on, "Quahadi do not have the white squaw's horse, but mebbeso we find it."

"We would appreciate that," said Hamilton. "All right, then, shall we call it a deal? Two beeves a week, and you leave the Yellowhouse canyon alone?"

But Newton's sudden, unexpected voice broke in. "I don't see no sense in paying blackmail!" He fingered the butt of his .54. "These damn' Indians are holding us up to the tune of two critters a week. That's all it amounts to." His face reddened with anger as he talked.

Clay said stubbornly, "In my opinion they have something coming."

"Ain't buffalo steak good enough for 'em?"

"I've et plenty of buffalo," Dow Jones put in, "and I

11

never saw anything wrong with it."

Quanah Parker's strong voice broke through their vociferous talk. "The Quahadi has always depended on the buffalo for food and shelter, but for the last ten years the herds have been getting smaller."

"We got nothin' to do with that," Dow Jones said belligerently.

Quanah looked grimly at him. "The white man built a great railroad across the prairies. Since then the buffalo have been in two herds—one north, one south. The south herd ranges here, in the land of the Quahadi."

Newton snorted. "There's plenty of shaggies. I seen 'em up on the Plains the other day."

Quanah Parker drew a deep breath that spoke of patience nearing a limit. "Each spring the calves are fewer because the buffalo has less grass. And now the white hunters are coming into Quahadi country to kill for hides."

"There's a treaty of Medicine Lodge"—Newton spoke sarcastically, as if he were dealing with a man trying to deceive him—"that keeps all white hunters north of the Arkansas River."

The impassive Quahadi braves at last shifted their feet, but Quanah Parker regarded Newton steadily. "By agreement," he said, "that was changed to the Cimarron River, because the whites were already across the Arkansas and my people wanted to avoid war. But the white hunters do not keep their word. This summer they have crossed the Cimarron like grasshoppers. They have killed buffalo by thousands; they take the hide but they leave the meat to rot in the sun. The Plains are fouled with the stinking carcasses, the sky is black with buzzards, and the air is filled with flies. In a few years there will be no buffalo, and the Quahadi will go hungry."

"That's up in the northern part of the Panhandle," Tompkins said thoughtfully. "There's nothing we can do about that."

"There are many piles of bones on the Plains above the Caprock." Quanah pointed to the southwest. "Many fresh kills. Not by Indians. Not by comancheros—for only the hides are taken. And there are no ranchers except in this canyon."

No one answered that charge, and Quanah seemed to draw himself up and grow taller and grimmer. "There will be much trouble," he declared. "Many scalps will be taken."

Newton said in a menacing drawl, "Is that a declaration of war?"

Quanah Parker answered, "I came in peace. I go in peace. But my people cannot live on prairie dogs."

"I won't agree to blackmail," Newton said ominously, "not even if somebody else pays the bill. Raid and be damned!" he burst out with startling violence. "I'll cut the heart out of every redskin that puts a moccasin on my place."

Quanah looked at Clay Hamilton, who shook his head. Parker took a deep breath. "Sorry," he said, and turned in dignity, his feather trains swirling. He jumped lightly onto his horse and started off at a walk, his war bonnet bobbing.

Newton's huge .54 came up, drawing a bead on Quanah Parker's back. But Hamilton knocked his arm down hard. "That's murder," he said harshly.

"You're a fool." Newton's voice was thick with fury. "One shot could end this whole dirty business. That half-breed Parker puts the Comanches up to all this. What's an Indian anyway," he argued, "but an animal?"

13

He watched the departing Comanches. They had not looked back. "You can smell 'em from here," he said. "If they were human beings, they wouldn't stink."

Hamilton said immovably, "They're human beings—and when human beings face starvation, nobody *has* to put them up to anything."

Newton glared at him but slowly put away his pistol. They watched the Indians' horses. splash back across the Yellowhouse.

Tompkins said speculatively: "He's right about one thing: the comancheros put the Indians up to a lot of this raiding. Maybe we ought to get up a posse and clean out the comancheros first."

Dow Jones spoke up. "That means going up on the Plains—and you can see how the Comanches feel about *that*."

CHAPTER 2

BEHIND THE HITCH RACK, SITTING ON THE SMALL front step of the big dobe ranch house when the first shot had sounded from the Caprock, was Madeline Hamilton, slim-built, russet-eyed, and of medium height. Her hair was a deep brown that revealed red lights in the sun; it was full and long, and she wore it in two glossy braids, one on each side.

She was restless, for she was accustomed to taking part in her father's activities. She had been the only woman on that frontier for a number of years, and as Clay's daughter and heir to the Tres Casas Ranch she had ridden constantly at her father's side. At his urging she had made it her business to know cattle and to understand ranching problems, for the Tres Casas, while not a big outfit compared to some, still comprised seven sections of good grass in a sheltered, watered valley, and was one of the finest properties in West Texas. Her father had advised her that because of the violence of frontier life she might at any time be forced to operate the ranch herself, and Madeline wanted to be ready.

Today, for the first time within her memory, her father had excluded her, because, as he said, the Indians would not powwow with a woman. Though she had understood, she had not known what to do with herself, and had sat self-consciously on the step, watching and listening.

She too had been alarmed by Shorty's signal, and she had watched the Caprock, shading her eyes with a slim, capable white hand.

Shorty's left arm was half paralyzed from a rattlesnake bite, and the big gray was head-shy enough to keep backing away until Shorty hit on the right combination of profanity, unless, of course, a band of Kiowas or Cheyennes was swooping down on him, in which event Shorty would be hunting cover. She suspected that Shorty had lost his temper and kicked the gray, and that it would be several minutes before they would be drinking out of the same hat, so she had leaned back against the dobe, carefully scanning the legendary Caprock, not immediately concerned but nevertheless alert.

The Caprock was a layer of gravel and clay and heavily alkalized dirt that formed the flat top surface of the great Llano Estacado above them. Beneath the Caprock, all around the Llano, occasional rain and the constant driving wind kept the softer formations eroded almost vertically, so that there were no sloping approaches to the Llano. Instead, the edge of the great

15

plain appeared to be a layer, several hundred feet thick, pushed straight up out of the earth by some weird and tremendous force. There was, of course, no way a wagon could mount the escarpment, and it was only by a few steep, precarious trails that a saddled horse could climb its sides. And at this moment, as Madeline watched, the ragged, vertical cliffs in the shadows of the late afternoon sun exhibited the endless range of bottomless browns and mysterious purples that seemed to support the Llano's fabled inaccessibility.

The Yellowhouse fork—farther down the stream they called it the Double Mountain fork—of the Brazos flowed southeast through the canyon by the Hamilton ranch house. It came down from the Llano two miles above as a small stream that became even smaller in the summer—as it had particularly during this summer of 1873. Near the Hamilton place, however, it was augmented by the outpouring of large twin springs, around which Clay had built his outfit.

The canyon at this point was less than a mile wide, filled with solid areas of gray-green sagebrush. Against the Caprock walls a few stunted, dark-green cedar trees grew. The north wall offered protection from blizzard weather, and against that wall Clay had built four corrals and a horse barn, a saddle-and-harness shed, a feed-storage barn, and an outhouse. Then he had dug a large cellar and built a two-story dobe over it. There was a pleasant grove of cottonwoods bordering the stream from the point where the springs rose, at the base of the north wall, to where it joined the creek, about a quarter of a mile away; and in the open, halfway between the ranch house and the river, was the big old cottonwood tree.

She observed all this, at the same time watching for

signs of Indian hostility but seeing none. That was not particularly reassuring, for the Comanches were adept at invisible movement through the sparse vegetation of the Panhandle. Then came Wilbarger's announcement. Following Shorty's signal, she saw the wagon and wondered why a newcomer was driving up the Yellowhouse when there was no *puerta* in the region.

As she watched the moving dust cloud that slowly resolved itself into a wagon, she remembered the day her father and mother had come up the same trail eight years before. Her father had ridden a buckskin gelding, and her mother had driven an ox team hitched to a covered wagon, while Madeline herself had alternately ridden double with her father and on the hard wooden seat in the jolting, swaying wagon beside her mother.

Her father, a Confederate captain, had gone home from the war in 1865 to their small ranch in Tom Green County. Their cattle had multiplied during the war years, but so had everyone else's, and there was no way to get them to market. All were cattle-poor, and there was no money with which to buy land or to lease grazing rights. There was talk of trail drives, but Indian Territory lay to the north, and was risky. So Clay Hamilton rounded up his rangy longhorns and moved out past the frontier, into Comanche country, up toward the Llano Estacado, where scouts told of swift streams and deep-grass valleys grazed only by antelope and buffalo. That had been in 1866, and though Clay Hamilton's neighbors in the Fort Concho area had predicted quick extermination of his family by the savages, he had found this sheltered valley and had driven up it. Then one day they had seen the big cottonwood, and Clay Hamilton had said, "This is where we'll build."

They had settled there between the springs and the tree, and tried to learn how to live in a new and different country, a land of drought and driving wind, of dust and dirt, of prairie fires and sudden northers. There had been years of work, of hoofs drumming on hard earth, the smell of saddles soaked in horse sweat, the creak of leather on the back of a bucking horse, bawling calves at roundup time, and the stench of burned hair under a red branding iron.

There had been the summer when the buckskin gelding became addicted to pink locoweed and trampled Madeline's mother to death, and Madeline remembered the trouble they'd had finding enough wood to make a coffin, for every usable log of any size in the valley had gone into corrals. The neighbors who had settled below the Hamilton place thought she should be buried in a blanket; but when Clay started trimming down the logs from his corral for planks, they got together and donated the sideboards from their wagons so that she could be buried properly up near the springs.

It had been a new and violent country, but they had not been alone for long. In 1867 Gordon Gault had arrived, a sallow-faced young man with hard blue eyes who never offered information about his past. He had thinning brown hair with little gloss, a concave face, and a mouth that turned down at the corners; but when he talked to a woman, or at least when he talked to Madeline—for after her mother died Madeline was the only white woman between Fort Griffin, 150 miles east, and Fort Bascom, far to the west in New Mexico Territory—the corners of his mouth turned up, his eyes seemed to soften, and his voice lost some of its metallic quality. He talked pleasantly and sometimes even a little wistfully—but never about himself.

He had settled below them in the canyon, and presently, having started, as her father said, "with a couple of heifers, a rope and a brandin' iron," he presently had a fair-sized bunch of cows. Those were times when men took sides broadly. A man was a ranchman, an Indian, a Mexican, or an outlaw. If he was a ranchman, then other ranchmen were not too fussy about unbranded stock so long as he paid his bills and could be depended upon to help fight Indians. The only criticism her father had made of Gordon Gault was the dry remark, "I'd like to get my hands on half a dozen heifers as prolific as his."

Following Gault, and filling up the canyon where it began to widen out, had come others, the men out there now under the cottonwood. There was Tompkins, another Confederate officer—tall and capable. Tompkins always wore a .36 caliber Colt that he had brought home from the war.

There was Dow Jones, a wizened little man from Georgia, with one eye socket empty because of a bayonet thrust; he wore wooly sheepskin chaps to protect a bad leg.

There was the long-mustached Newton with his clumsy old .54 Navy pistol and a powder horn always hanging from his left shoulder. He was a hothead, but so far he had given no trouble.

There was the black-hatted Wilbarger. He had been a Texas ranger and had fought Mexicans along the Rio Grande, and he still carried a long bowie knife in a leather sheath. "It takes a man to handle it," he said once, "but it shore whittles 'em down to a size."

There were MacLeod and Campbell, both Scotsmen, both big and broad, who had come down from Canada last spring.

19

These were the men who had settled along the Yellowhouse on the broad secondary plains below the forbidding Caprock. They were hardy men and accustomed to danger.

Madeline heard the mention of comancheros, and was alert at once. She felt that the comancheros were fundamentally responsible for the theft of the blue roan stallion, which was a personal loss and hard to accept; but what worried her most about the horse was the fact that, though the roan was gentle and affectionate, he was also spirited and proud. When he was treated understandingly he was magnificent, but when he was treated harshly he was immovably stubborn. All the comancheros she had seen were either sly or uncouth, harsh fellows who would not give a second thought to understanding a horse like the blue roan; at his first sign of spirit they would apply the whip. The thought made her wince.

As the Comanches, in full ceremonial dress, stopped at the cottonwood, she moved quietly up to a freight-wagon that stood a little forward of the house, almost even with the hitch rack. The wagon had just been brought back from Breckenridge with supplies for the coming year, and the long plaited rawhide bullwhip was still coiled about the right-hand front corner stake of the wagon box. Madeline sat down on the doubletree and watched her father and the other ranchmen move up to the cottonwood. It came to her with a start that of them all, Gordon Gault had not yet spoken. He was the one man she'd be afraid to ride the river with. She never knew what he was thinking. She watched him now, walking with his hard, almost arrogant stride.

He wore a vest of reddish-brown calfskin, the collar

and pockets of which were widely edged with purple velvet that was not very clean. The back of his neck was always fiery red from the sun, for he was a man who didn't brown. His face was shaded by a big dove-gray hat, his hands were protected by gloves, and the back of his neck was the only skin exposed. As she watched, he looked downvalley toward the distant wagon of the comanchero. Madeline thought it strange that when the chief of the Quahadi and eleven of his warriors were in the yard, and it was possible to be caught between two fires, Gault should seem more immediately concerned about a comanchero than about the Indians, and she wondered why.

She remembered when her father and Tompkins had first discussed the idea of a powwow. Her father had said, "We ought to try making an agreement with them before we start killing them."

"Or before they start killing us," Tompkins had said. "For that matter, we'd better be mighty careful if we do meet them. They don't like whites; they might use the meeting to try to wipe us out. And remember, they're Comanches. They don't always kill quick."

"I know that," her father said soberly, "and I know how they dislike the whites; but the Indians haven't had much of a square deal from the white man so far, and I'd like to start treating them like human beings. They say this Quanah Parker keeps his word, so I figure a powwow under a truce is a chance worth taking. It might save a lot of killing."

Now, as she watched them palaver, heard their words, heard Newton's explosive ultimatum, and saw the Indians turn and leave, she felt sorry for her father, for she knew how much he had wanted to settle their differences peacefully. With one thing she agreed: the comancheros were at the bottom of the trouble. She liked Quanah Parker; he was an Indian, but he was a man, and he looked like an honest man. She felt very strongly that if it were not for the comancheros there would be no trouble with the Comanches, and it seemed clear enough that the way to settle their Indian troubles was to run the comancheros off the Plains.

CHAPTER 3

WILBARGER BROKE A LITTLE AWAY FROM THE GROUP. He looked toward the hitch rack where their horses were standing, then started in that direction. His movements were smooth and liquid; his walk always seemed catlike in spite of the high-instepped boots that threw most men out of balance. His soft leather chaps slapped noisily, and the long knife swung a little with his steps. Then he stopped to look down the valley, and seemed to reconsider. He stood facing downstream. He fished in his vest pockets for makings, and began to build a cigarette.

Newton went over and flopped down on the cottonwood root beside Dow Jones and began to talk vehemently, digging furrows in the earth with the buck hooks on his spurs.

Clay Hamilton stood where he was, watching the Indians steadily drawing away up the opposite side of the Yellowhouse, toward the head of the canyon. The Indians were out of pistol range, but Hamilton kept one eye on Newton. MacLeod and Campbell stood beside him. So did Tompkins.

Wilbarger raised his right knee to tighten the seat of his pants, drew a match across it sharply, then held the

22

match at arm's length. The match smoldered for a moment, as they always did, emitting clouds of blue smoke and a sharp smell of sulphur that reached Madeline almost at once on the steady breeze blowing up the valley. Then the match burst into flame, and Wilbarger cupped his hands around it to light his brown-papered cigarette.

Gordon Gault, his tall hat nodding with the unevenness of his walk in the high-heeled boots, came past Wilbarger toward Madeline. He looked nice when he smiled, and she smiled back. He cut a wide circle around the heels of a rangy bay that stood with head down at the end of the hitch rack.

"How's the pinto coming along?" he asked.

She slapped her fringed gauntlet gloves against her soft, ankle-length, buckskin leather skirt, thinking it was odd that Gault did not seem concerned about the ominous result of the meeting with the Indians. "Too slow," she said, looking back toward the corral. "Father won't let me ride him yet; he's afraid something might happen to spoil him. In the meantime I'm riding the bay there." She nodded at the hitch rack. "He's a good roping horse, but that's all he knows. He'll back over the Caprock some day."

"A good roping horse is supposed to back."

"I know that," she said. "I was born in a sidesaddle. But the bay works too hard at it."

He glanced at her divided skirt and then at the saddle on the bay. "You don't ride sidesaddle now," he observed.

"I haven't ridden sidesaddle since mother died. You can't do cutting and roping sitting on a piano bench."

They were walking toward the big corral on the higher ground behind the house. The corral was built like a very heavy rail fence about ten feet high, with peeled cottonwood logs serving as crosspieces, and tied to the upright posts with strips of rawhide that had hardened like iron in the sun. In the corral now were half a dozen working-horses, but Madeline and Gault went around it.

A narrow chute connected the big corral to the bronc corral, with peeled branches thrust through from the side of the chute to the other to serve as a gate. The bronc corral also was high-sided, but was small and made differently, with a fence of various-length branches planted upright in the ground and leaning outward at the top like a solid picket fence about to fall over. They walked around the bronc pen to a third, medium-sized corral made like the first, of heavy upright posts, heavy crosspieces, and rawhide lashings. This pen was also ten feet high and about forty feet in diameter, and connected to both of the others by chutes. A snubbing post was set in the center, and near the post a glossy black-and-white gelding was nibbling at a broken bale of hay.

Madeline kicked cautiously along the ground under the bottom rail with the toe of her boot. "I can usually kick out a rattler or two," she explained. "They like to sun themselves there in the afternoon." She added, "There's none there now, though."

She put one foot on the bottom rail, thrust her head through an open space between two rails, and leaned on both elbows. Gault followed her, but the rail above knocked his hat to the back of his head. He looked at her quickly. She laughed. He laughed, took off his hat, stuck his head through, then his arms, and finally stood beside her, slapping his hat gently against the inside of the corral. The gelding had heard them and looked up.

"Don't scare him," Madeline warned. "Father would have a fit."

"Scare *him*?" he asked. "*I'm* the one to be scared."

He looked sidewise at her. He was big-chested and big-shouldered, and made more bulky by the reddish-brown calfskin vest, and where the space between the logs was ample for her, it made a snug fit for Gault. He laughed again as his neck scraped audibly against the upper log; the sound was like that of a knife scraping the hair off a butchered hog. She laughed back, but, conscious of his closeness and the fact that he was talking about himself but thinking about her, she was suddenly uneasy and cut her laugh short.

He looked at the gelding. "Mighty nice piece of horseflesh," he said. "There's nothing wrong with Clay Hamilton's eye."

The gelding took a step toward them. It walked, Madeline thought, with the same liquid grace that Wilbarger displayed. Its muscles seemed to flow under the glossy skin. Madeline nodded. "He'll be all right, but he isn't the horse the blue roan stallion was." She added pensively. "I'll never forgive myself for turning him out to grass the night the Indians came down."

He looked at her from the corner of his eye. "You liked that stallion, didn't you?"

"I'd give anything to have him back," she said. "I could rope a steer on that horse; but the gelding here hasn't got enough weight."

He looked at her a little doubtfully. "Roping steers is pretty heavy work, ma'am."

"I can do anything on the ranch," she said, "except keep house. I was too young for that when Mother died, and Father has always taken me out on the range with him since then."

She was suddenly quiet, looking downvalley. The dust cloud, which had left the marsh now, was a little larger, and crawling steadily upstream. The ranchmen were still under the big cottonwood. Wilbarger was talking to her father, the cigarette dangling erratically from his lips, his big black hat perched on the back of his head.

From where Madeline and Gault stood on the upper side of the training corral, they could see to their right the small stream that carried water from the two springs down to the Yellowhouse—about as much as could flow swiftly through a hogshead. Ahead and a little to their left was the ranch house, with its back door opening toward them. It was a good-sized building, and the hands bunked on the second floor. There were five cowboys and a cook, besides Shorty, who did the harness work, grubbed mesquite roots for the kitchen range, filled kerosene lamps, and did other odd jobs around the ranch. In front of the house was the long hitch rack; past the house was the big cottonwood, and, fifty yards farther on, the spring water flowed into the Yellowhouse.

Madeline backed away from the fence to look up the canyon. The Indians had not had time to reach the head of the canyon, but they had disappeared from sight, to her relief. She turned back and surprised an unpleasant gleam in Gault's blue eyes. He had clapped his hat on and was looking up the canyon too.

"You don't like Indians, do you?"

He said coldly, "I believe with General Sheridan that a dead Indian is a good Indian."

"I feel sorry for them myself," she said, to prod him into talking. "They live according to their own ideas, but so do we. And this was their country first. You can't deny that."

"Who had it before them?" he snapped. "They took it away from somebody else, didn't they?"

She said softly, "What have the Indians done to you?"

He turned to her with a glare in his eyes that made her take a backward step. "In 1849," he said, "my mother took me with her in a wagon and chasséd for California—never mind where we came from. My old man was a sailor, and never came back after I was born, but my mother figured there was gold in California and she might as well have some of it. We followed the Santa Fe Trail. We didn't have much grub, so we took the Cimarron Cutoff. It was a small train. We hit Ute Creek, and a band of Jicarilla Apaches set fire to the train and killed everybody but the kids." He shook his big head. "My mother died with six arrows in her chest." He was looking upcanyon. "They sold me to the Paiutes as a slave, but I got away and came back here."

She looked up at him. "Want to get even?" she asked.

He looked down at her. "I'll get even, but not by killing." There was a curious light in his eyes. "I'll let the Army do my killing."

She noted the momentary hunched attitude of his shoulders, and guessed that it was caused by the memory of many whippings, for she had no doubt he had been a truculent captive. She was moved, and said gently: "You mustn't be bitter. That's all over. This is a new life—a new country. The grass is free, the sky is clear, and the air is good."

She had moved a half-step closer to him, and looked down the canyon, moved by the grandeur of the great escarpment with its long, deep blue shadows now reaching from the western Caprock to the bottom of the Yellowhouse valley.

She turned to him and saw that he too was moved. He was looking down at her with a new light in his sallow face. For the first time since she had known him, she thought she was seeing the man beneath the hard, defensive glaze in his pale blue eyes.

"Miss Madeline," he said, "let's get married."

The abruptness of his words was a shock to her. She stared at him, amazed and incredulous. She was startled to realize that this new attitude took something from the strength that had always appeared in his aloofness, and with this seeming weakness her old distrust, and even occasional dislike of him, welled up in her instantaneously. She turned her head away, knowing that he would be able to read her eyes. Perhaps her feelings were unjustified, but they were there. Because she didn't want to hurt him, she turned away until they had passed.

For a moment the only sound was the bubbling of the stream past the corral; then, across the Yellowhouse, she heard a prairic dog yip. She turned back and said carefully, "I'll have to have a chance to make some medicine for that question, Gault." She looked full at him then, and saw an eager look in his eyes.

He began to talk earnestly: "Your father's Three Houses brand takes care of the valley two miles up and two miles down. My stuff runs three miles more downstream, and beyond that the canyon begins to widen out. Do you see what that means?"

She looked at him blankly.

"Your father's brand and mine control the Yellowhouse up here," he said, his eyes shining. "If a drought comes, we'd have first call on the water; also, it gives us control of the Plains area around here. The head of this canyon is the only place within fifty miles

28

where they could build a road up to the Llano, and all we'd have to do to control traffic on a road like that would be to get legal title to a strip of land across the canyon. That makes plenty of savvy, doesn't it?"

She saw what he meant then, and she knew why the light in his eyes had repelled her: it was that of avarice and not of love. She had hardly expected a romantic proposal, for men of the frontier were not given to fine words; but she had thought, once the words were said, he would be more at ease, and would say something to indicate he wanted her because she was a woman. She would have cherished that—but he was talking business. Madeline faced the bitter hurt that Gault wanted her for the land she represented—and she would find it hard to forgive him for that.

She became alert, seeing his words as they were, looking for meanings behind them. Not quite sure of her ground, she looked up at him. "The Tres Casas already controls the upper canyon."

"What if something happened to your father?"

She began to stiffen. "If anything happens to my father," she said, "then *I* will control the upper canyon."

It made him pause. The hardness began to come back into his eyes. "An unmarried girl running a ranch," he said, "would be a target for every shyster in the country."

For a moment she knew fear—a kind she had not known before. The fear of animals and Indians and weather hazards she was used to, but she did not know how to cope with the cold calculation that had prompted him to propose marriage to her. She knew at that moment that if she should be left alone with the ranch, Gault would stop at nothing to take it away from her. If she married him she would be safe, surrounded by his coldness. If she stood alone, he would fight her with all the cunning in his brain.

But her voice was cold as she answered. "You're bettin' against me with my money, Gault."

His eyes became fully hard. "Call your shot," he said harshly.

She did. "The way it is now, my father and I already have the head of the canyon. You're trying to buy in with nothing, just the way you bought yourself into the ranching business when you came here, Gault."

His face turned white. His jaws knotted at the corners. "You're lucky, ma'am," he said in a hard, metallic voice. "No man alive could say that to me and live."

She had talked bluntly but she had spoken the truth, and with that knowledge her fear lessened, and she said quietly, "You showed your hand, Gault." She stopped, puzzled again, but he did not answer, and she went on: "I don't know exactly why you want the head of the canyon anyway, Gault, unless it's got something to do with the Indians. That doesn't add up right, because you hate Indians, but you said something about using them. You want the upper canyon so you'll have free access to the Llano. I see that. It isn't so easy for you to go up on the Llano from the place where you are now, without everybody knowing. If you were up here on this place, you could get up on the Llano without anybody knowing. But why, Gault? Surely not for a few buffalo hides that you can hardly afford to pack home."

She was aghast at the change that came over him. His white face turned as red as the back of his neck. His chest swelled and his hard blue eyes blazed. He started to speak, but no sound came out. He swallowed, and when at last the words came, they were charged with venom. "When a lady takes a man's place," he said ominously, "she better expect a man's treatment."

"I can take care of myself," she said coolly.

His jaw worked, and her fear surged back. She realized the tremendous power of the big man, and the violence of his hatred. She had gone too far, and he had openly threatened her; she knew what he meant by her taking a man's place, and she knew now there was no reasoning with him. Gordon Gault was a dangerous man, a man who would not be stopped by the traditional frontier respect for a woman, because he had no tradition behind him. Reading the malevolence in his eyes, she knew with chilling certainty that he was stopped from harming her now only by the presence of the men under the cottonwood.

For the first time in her life she was weak with relief when he wheeled and stalked away. Suddenly she felt no longer self-sufficient. She had what she considered a childish urge to tell her father, but that was gone in a moment, for she knew that Gault had not said anything that, repeated by someone else, amounted to more than a proposal of marriage for business reasons. She knew, too, that if her father should take it up it would end in death. She walked back to the freight wagon and sat again on the doubletree, slapping her gloves against her leather skirt, and watched Gault join her father and the others.

Tompkins looked at Gault sharply. "You're the gent's been killing buffalo up on the Llano," he said.

Gault looked truculent. He was taller and heavier than any of them, and he didn't back down. "They didn't carry *your* brand," he said pointedly.

Tompkins answered, "They didn't carry yours either."

Wilbarger observed, "The Indians have to eat."

31

"Who said they have to eat?" Gault asked stonily.

Clay Hamilton said quickly: "You're making trouble for us, Gault. What do you want to kill buffalo for anyway? There aren't enough on this part of the Llano as it is."

"For one thing," Gault said, "I can sell the hides. For another thing, if there's no buffalo up there, there won't be any Indians around here. They'll have to leave."

Wilbarger asked, "Where are you selling hides? I haven't seen any stacked up around your place."

"I agree with Gault," said Newton, rising. "Kill off the buffalo and you get shut of the redskins."

"Where can the Indians go?" asked Hamilton. "The Llano is the last place in the country."

"Who cares where they go?" Gault asked coldly.

"It'd be a right smart thing to get them off the Llano," Dow Jones observed from his seat on the cottonwood root. "It's only a question of time until we've got to take our cattle up there. This valley down here won't handle any more stock than we've got in it. What are we going to feed our calves next spring?"

"There's good grass up on the Llano," said Campbell. "I've been up there myself. Some places it's knee-high."

"I've been up there too," Hamilton said. "Up on the Plains the Yellowhouse runs pretty dry unless it rains—and it doesn't rain very often."

"There's supposed to be a big spring somewhere between here and the New Mexico line," Dow Jones reminded them, "but they say the Indians plugged it up with rocks."

Newton exploded. "The dirty redskins! They did that just to keep us from finding it."

"Well," said Hamilton, looking at the Caprock, "I don't reckon I want to be the first one to go up there.

That's the last stronghold of the Plains Indians; they'll be hard to whip.

Campbell said, "No doot aboot it—but what are we to do if the grasshoppers come up the Yellowhouse? This summer they were all over Texas, and they do say all the way north to Canada—the worst they've ever been. If they come up this valley and destroy the grass, whats left for us to do but go up on the Plains?"

Tompkins looked up. "If they come from the east, the Caprock might stop them at that," he noted. He looked at Clay Hamilton. "We may be *forced* to go up there."

There was a pause. The voice of the mule skinner down the valley came to them, talking mule language.

Hamilton shook his head. "There's still the Indians," he reminded them.

Wilbarger spoke up. "I rode into Fort Griffin when I went after supplies this summer, and talked to the Army men about it. They figure just the way we said: it isn't as much the Indians' fault as it is the comancheros'. Colonel Mackenzie says the Indians wouldn't bother us if they didn't have the comancheros to trade with."

Campbell asked, "Why doesn't the Army establish regulations?"

Wilbarger answered. "That isn't easy. The comancheros don't pay much attention to other people's rules; they make their own law—what little they observe. But that ain't the worst of it. If the comancheros traded on their own it might not be so bad, but Mackenzie says they're organized. He figgers there's a white man somewhere who furnishes the money for them to operate on, then tips them off when and where to raid the ranches; they tip off the Indians; then he takes most of the profit without any risk. The traders aren't savers anyway; all they want is enough to

33

get drunk on. Mackenzie figgers if he could uncover the feller who furnishes the money and does the spying, he could break it up. And if they break up that trade, the Indian trouble will dry up."

"One company of Texas Rangers," Tompkins observed, "could clean up the whole Panhandle."

"The Rangers were disbanded during the war," Wilbarger reminded him.

Clay Hamilton was watching Wilbarger closely. "What's the colonel going to do about it?"

"He said there'd probably be an Army detachment sent out from Fort Griffin this fall."

Gault moved forward and said loudly: "I say we should keep the Army out of it. We came up here and settled this country, and we've taken care of things by ourselves up to now. If the Army comes in here we'll be living the way they tell us to. You know that yourself. Anyway," he argued, "I've scouted the Plains up there looking for water, and I never found any signs of comancheros causing trouble. I figure the Indians are out for blood—especially white blood. They're killers, and everybody knows it. They'd rather kill than eat any day."

Madeline heard his speech with some astonishment, for Gault usually said little, but now he had spoken long and positively. She took exception to his position, too, for she had long felt strongly with her father about the Indians and their rights. She wanted to defend her father, and now that Quanah Parker's party was gone there was no reason why she should not. She got up and went toward the group. She also believed that the comancheros were responsible for much of the Indian trouble, and she chose that avenue to oppose Gault. "It seems to me," she said, "that the ranchmen themselves are at fault. These comancheros have to bring their goods in wagons or mule packs, don't they?"

"Yes, ma'am," said Wilbarger.

"All right. Then they have to travel over our land. Why don't we organize the ranchers all around the Llano and keep them off the Plains? Keep them out of the country?"

"Most of them come in from the Now Mexico side," Wilbarger said.

"Those who come in from this side we can stop," she insisted.

Tompkins said gently: "We don't own but very little of the land, Miss Madeline—just about what our ranch houses are on, you might say. The rest of it is all free range. We have no right to keep a man from driving across it, as long as he doesn't do us any harm."

"They *are* doing us harm!" she said. "Why fight the Indians when we can clean up the whole trouble by removing the cause? I say we must take care of the comancheros first. We must keep them off the Plains."

"We can't stop them, Miss Madeline."

"Why not?" she demanded, impatient with the men who faced the issue so clearly but seemed so helpless to do anything about it. She caught her father's warning glance, and knew she was on the verge of rashness; but she saw Gault's pale blue eyes on her, and the unflattering recollection of his cold proposal and greedy reasoning roused her incautious, driving spirit. She said hotheadedly, "As long as we have whips we can stop them."

Newton's drawl came instantly. "This is a mighty good time to try that out, ma'am. That there wagon is comin' up the valley, and it's pulled by four mules. If that ain't a trader headed for the Plains, I miss my guess."

Aghast, she realized the full import of her words, and for a moment she detested Newton, who was always quick to encourage trouble. But she faced the fact that she had asked for it. She turned to stare at the approaching prairie wagon with its unusually high sides. Four small Spanish mules were drawing it steadily up the canyon, and now they were less than a quarter of a mile away. She noted the man on horseback, a little ahead and at one side so his dust would not cross the wagon. She noted his horse, and gasped, for the moment forgetting her violent words.

"That horse has a golden coat!" she said. "And white mane and tail."

Clay Hamilton nodded. "That's a California sorrel," he said quickly, as if to divert attention from her rash statement. "Don't see many of 'em up here. Right nice piece of buzzard bait that gent is ridin'."

She was grateful to her father. He never refused to back her play, but he usually showed her a way out. Then she saw a movement of Gordon Gault's reddish vest, and she turned his way. He was watching her from his cold blue eyes, and his concave face was derisive. She felt her anger rise. He turned to the approaching wagon, and said without looking at her, "Are you going to turn him back, ma'am, or shall I?"

Her father looked at Gault and frowned. Tompkins cleared his throat. Wilbarger toyed with the butt of his knife. Dow Jones began, "I don't think—"

But there was something in the wizened man's voice . . . or did she imagine it? Did the others, too, think she was trading on her privileges as a woman, taking a man's rights without assuming a man's responsibilities? Her pride flared. Her face grew hot.

36

She turned haughtily. Her father moved to stop her; the eyes of all the men were on her. She shrugged away from her father. She strode to the freight wagon and seized the coiled bullwhip from the wagon stake. Then she grasped the reins of the bay, tossed one under his neck and back over his mane, got them both in her left hand, put her foot in the stirrup, grasped the saddle horn with her left hand, and swung her leather skirt over the cantle. The bay was wheeling toward her. She sank into the saddle and ground her spurs into his ribs. He lunged forward and made for the Yellowhouse at a gallop.

CHAPTER 4

THE BAY'S HOOFS WHIPPED THE SHALLOW WATER OF the stream. She turned him to the left and drew him down to a lope. Her face was still burning, but she was determined. The hardminded men back under the cottonwood had to be shown that she was capable of doing her own work. She knew that now, after her reckless talk, she would have to prove up to hold their respect.

She rode down on the stranger and his wagon. The schooner had no hoops but was loaded heavily, with a tarpaulin lashed over the top and halfway down the high sides. The beautiful California sorrel was stepping along easily, holding its head up and lifting its white-booted legs high. A pair of rawhide hobbles hung from its neck in traditional Texas fashion. It blew the dust out of its throat and shook its head, and the white mane rippled in the softening sunlight.

Madeline drew up on the stranger's right, noting the gun at his right thigh, and sat the bay down into a full stop, careful to keep him parallel with the stranger's horse so that she would not be hidden by the bay's head. The stranger stopped. He was a tall, thin man, weather-worn and wiry, and sat lightly in the saddle; it was near the end of the day, but the sorrel still looked fresh, with the darkness of sweat barely showing under the ornamented edge of the corona—a high recommendation for the rider. The man wore a tall hat of light brown, a red bandanna handkerchief around his neck, and a faded red-and-black-checked flannel shirt with an open vest of black-and-white-spotted wildcat hide. He had blue arm bands like her father's, and the gauntlets of a pair of buckskin gloves protruded from his right hip pocket.

He raised a lean brown hand to the brim of his tall hat, which had only a single crease down the front of the crown, where the ranchmen in the valley always wore three or four creases. He lifted his hat as if he never had been in a hurry in his life. "Howdy, ma'am," he said, and there was real pleasure in his clear, friendly voice. She looked at his face, and it held her for a moment. He had gray eyes like her father's and his face was neither young nor old. It could be a stern face, she thought, but now it was gentle and turning into the first makings of a smile. She looked straight into the gray eyes and saw honest warmth in them.

"Howdy, stranger," she said stiffly.

The sorrel stopped, and the wagon lumbered to a halt.

"Anything I can do for you, ma'am?"

He was still holding his hat in his hand, and his genuine friendliness, his warmth, seemed to dissolve her bitterness and dampen her determination to prove herself. The stranger's gray eyes were looking at her in a way she wasn't used to—the way of a man looking at

38

a woman—the way Gordon Gault had not looked at her. For a moment she reveled in it, and then she remembered that this man was a comanchero, and that she had only contempt for comancheros. She opened her challenge. "Have you seen a blue roan stallion," she asked, "with the Tres Casas brand on the right hip?" She sat straight in the saddle and watched him answer, looking for any sign of guilt on his own part.

He shook his head. "I'm real sorry. I've seen a lot of nice-lookin' steers this afternoon with the Three Houses plastered on 'em, but no blue roan stallion. I take it he was a right nice animal."

It was strange, the way she softened when he spoke. She answered before she knew what she was saying. "The best in the Yellowhouse valley," she said.

He put his hat back on his head and patted the sorrel's neck. "I know how you feel, ma'am, to lose a good horse; but that looks like a nice brute you're on."

She glanced down at the bay's head. "He's a good roping horse," she said, "but you might as well ride a mule. You can't pet him. You can't get close to him."

He smiled sympathetically. "There's nothing takes the place of a good horse," he agreed. He leaned forward in the saddle, and the sorrel started to move. "Got to be rollin'," he said. "Sun ain't gettin' any higher." He swung the sorrel's rear quarters around deftly and faced her. He touched his hatbrim. "Glad to have come across you, ma'am." His eyes now were taking her in warmingly. "I sure didn't expect to see a lady out here, ma'am—leastways not a pretty one. I figured this for a man's country."

It struck her wrong—perhaps because he had so neatly forestalled her intention to challenge him. She knew how to challenge a stranger; she had seen it done

39

many times. But this man didn't look like the kind you would or could run out of the valley with rude treatment. Then, too, he had given her a nice compliment—which she should have received from Gault but hadn't; it annoyed her to depend on a comanchero for compliments. She was also irked by the obvious understanding between the stranger and his horse, and by the beauty of the animal. Before she thought further, she blurted, "Where did you get that sorrel?" Instantly she regretted it; that question, asked of a stranger, was an insult anywhere on the range, and it hurt more because the abrupt change on his face showed disappointment in her.

Frostiness appeared in his gray eyes. "I don't really blame you, ma'am, for asking that question," he said, but went on reprovingly: "A man would know better, of course, but I can see how a lady might be taken with this little cow-horse so as to forget her range manners."

She stiffened. She had been doing impulsive things all day, and so far none of them had turned out right.

He smiled. "Dulce came from California, ma'am. I rode her all the way myself." His voice had a pleasant, softly nasal quality. He went on without changing his tone, "May I ask where you got that bullwhip?"

She had never heard a rebuff delivered with such gentleness, and it showed up her own rudeness. She noted that his eyes were unnecessarily bland, and her anger was aroused. He was entirely too clever; he was even starting to ask the questions. She had sparred with him long enough. She asked a question, and she was no longer beating around the bush. "Where are you going with this outfit, stranger?"

His posture in the saddle did not change, but the frostiness came back into his eyes. "That don't sound like a friendly question, ma'am. Maybe I was mistaken about this being a free country." He looked pointedly at the big cottonwood. "I reckon," he said, "this is a new custom I have to get used to—a bunch of gents sending out a lady to do their work. But to answer your question, ma'am, so's we don't misunderstand each other: I'm headed for Mucha Que."

She straightened as if a cold ramrod had been laid along her back. "What for?" she demanded.

"It does seem that I'm answerin' all the questions, ma'am, but so far I have no objection." He was watching the cottonwood. "It looks," he said dryly, "like you're going to have reinforcements, ma'am." She knew without looking around that it would be Gault, but the stranger did not seem perturbed. "I'll tell you a story, ma'am," he said, his eyes on the cottonwood, "and I'll make it short in case you're in a hurry." He squinted at the sun, now just about its own width above the Caprock.

"I had a little spread down near San Antone," he said. "I came back from the war and found lots of beef on the hoof—like everybody else. Pretty soon I trailed a herd to San Diego and got a good price. But on the way back from California I was slowed up some by Indian trouble and didn't get back till this summer. Then I found the grasshoppers had eaten me out. Took the paint off the barn, roughed up the handle of my pitchfork till I had to throw it way." He was watching the sorrel's ears. "I sold out, put most of my money into trade goods, and came up here to the Llano. I heard it was a good country and a man could make some money trading with the Indians."

She said, "You've come to the wrong place. You better turn around and go up to Las Lenguas."

He leaned on the big Mexican saddle horn. "I

41

understand there's a lot of Indians camped on Las Lenguas River, and they're restless. I decided to come this way."

"You can't get over the Caprock here."

He looked up at the formidable cliffs. "I think I can make it all right, ma'am."

Again she felt a change of emotion. She had treated him rudely, but he had shown no offense. He was still friendly and courteous, and her anger was ebbing away. She had to save her face, however, and she said abruptly, quickly, before Gault came within hearing: "Look, Mister, why don't you go back? The people around here don't like comancheros."

He asked quietly, "What's wrong with the comancheros?"

She heard Gault's big blaze-faced dun trotting up behind her. "You're going up there to trade Scotch whisky to the Indians for stolen horses," she accused, hoping to get a response that would provide the excuse for action.

"Ma'am," he said earnestly, "I can assure you that is not so. It is well known all over Texas that an Indian will give just as many horses for a gallon of thirty-five-cent corn likker as he will for the best imported stuff you can buy." There was no smile on his face. His gray eyes were taking in Gault, who had made the affront of riding up on the opposite of the California sorrel, putting the stranger between the two of them and hiding his own gun hand. Now Gault avoided the stranger's probing look and sat with his pale blue eyes fixed cynically on Madeline. The stranger said seriously, "I don't think that remark about stolen horses holds any water, ma'am, because they told me at Fort Griffin that there are fifty thousand wild mustangs between the Salt

Fork and the Palo Duro, and the Indians can run down a horse in half a day."

She felt a sharp, unexpected fear of trouble, and a sudden urge to avoid it. "They don't run down the wild horses," she said sharply, striving to elicit some sign of compromise so that Gault would not force gunplay, for Gault was known to be a fast man with a gun. "They come down here at night and take *our* stock."

The stranger eyed Gault. "It may be, ma'am, that the ranchers in the Yellowhouse valley don't fight Indians as well as they do travelers."

She saw Gault's face begin to whiten. She spoke peremptorily, even a little frantically, to the stranger, "Turn around and go back! Now!"

He seemed to draw a deep breath, and sat up straight. "I came up here to do a legal business, ma'am, and I inquired about the ownership of the land before I started up the valley. The way I hear it, all the land along this side of the Yellowhouse is public grazing land, and a peaceful citizen has a right to travel over it."

He was talking to her, but his gray eyes were watching Gault. She looked at Gault, expecting to see him go for his gun. But Gault was watching her, with his mouth slightly turned down at the corners. His pale blue eyes scanned her face, then his glance dropped to her saddle horn and the bullwhip. Under the goading of Gault's cynical eyes and the stubborn resistance of the stranger, as well as her desire to avoid shooting, she snatched up the whip. Her fingers closed around the loaded handle, then she threw the coils straight out behind her and brought the whip forward with all her force. The wide, three-foot-long rawhide snapper at the end of the whip was aimed for the stranger's face, but he shot his gauntleted left arm straight up at the elbow and intercepted the blow before it reached its peak.

The snapper wrapped itself around his forearm. She jerked back to free the whip. The bay felt the tightening of the rawhide, and sat back hard against the pull. She felt the handle slipping through her fingers.

She dropped the reins and seized the whipstock with both hands. The bay was still backing, and too late she realized she was being pulled from the saddle. She released the whip, but she was halfway out of the saddle on the off side. The bay shied nervously, and she lost her balance. She had a glimpse of the stranger leaning along the sorrel's neck. In the same movement he plucked his revolver from its holster with his thumb and forefinger and tossed it behind him without looking. Then he was off the sorrel, and took three long steps toward her. He tried to help her up.

"Sorry, ma'am," he said, "but when a lady tries to take a man's place—" He shook his head.

She was spitting dirt and dry grass out of her mouth. She glared at him, refusing his help, and got to her feet.

"I'm sorry, ma'am," he said again, and turned back to the sorrel. He put his right foot in the off stirrup. He grasped the horn with his right hand.

She sputtered incredulously through her outrage, "You don't even know which side of a horse to get on."

"Hold it, mister," came Gault's grating voice. He had ridden around behind the sorrel, and now he left the saddle and hit the ground with both feet. "I seen you hide behind your crow bait and toss your gun to your pardner so you wouldn't have to face up to hot lead," he said, "just before you pulled the lady into the dirt."

Madeline glanced back at the prairie wagon. For the first time she saw an old man with a glossy black beard in the seat. He was holding the reins, and also, now, a long-barreled Walker Colt aimed at Gault.

The stranger dropped the stirrup and faced Gault. "Rather," he said clearly, "so you wouldn't have any excuse to shoot me in the back."

Gault did not reach for his pistol. He launched a big fist at the stranger's face. The stranger weaved to one side, and there was a sharp crack as his fist landed on Gault's chin. There was a second crack as his other fist landed there.

Gault backed away, shaking his head. The stranger went after him, but Gault was guarding his face. He straightened up and they traded blows. Once again Gault's face was as red as his neck. His hat rolled in the dirt. He charged the stranger. They went down, Gault on top. They were almost under the sorrel's belly, but the horse didn't move. They fought furiously on the ground.

The stranger planted a dusty, booted foot on Gault's chest and sent him staggering back, then leaped to his feet and launched himself at Gault. The stranger's hat was on the ground under the sorrel. Madeline picked the hat up automatically, without taking her eyes off the two men. Gault was heavier, and she assumed he would get the best of it; she was wondering now how it could end without shooting. She was even wondering how it had started without shooting, for ranchmen were not fist fighters. But the stranger was different. Even his hat was different; it was soft in her fingers, a fine piece of felt, lightly and closely woven, the kind a man could sleep on all night and then shake out the next morning without a wrinkle. That was not unusual, but it had a small band of daintily woven gold wire around the crown. She straightened out the felt and brushed the dirt from it.

Gault was boring in with his weight. The stranger

went backward. He fell. Gault's face was purple. He jumped at the stranger's face with both booted feet. The stranger rolled, caught Gault's legs, and tried to pull himself up. Gault hit him in the face, again and again. The stranger went limp.

Madeline's breath caught for an instant. Then she cried sharply, "Gault! That's enough."

Gault raised his head slowly. He had the eyes of a locoed horse, blazing with wild fury. But he got hold of himself. His hand twitched toward the gun still in his holster. The knots worked at the corners of his jaws. He looked at the whiskered man on the wagon seat, then he looked down at the stranger, who was stirring a little. Gault kicked him in the stomach, and went for his hat.

Madeline cringed. Painfully she watched the stranger drag himself to a sitting position. His face was bloody, and dirt and grass were mixed with blood on his left temple. He brushed it off, clumsily at first. Then he took a deep, ragged breath and got to his feet. He shook his head and looked around. His fingers found the sorrel's reins.

"Here's your hat, mister," said Madeline in an unsteady voice.

He took it. He smiled, and, incredibly, there was no malice in the smile. It was as warm and friendly as it had been when she first rode up. She was sorry now— sorry and ashamed—and she would have liked to tell him so, but she could not, with Gault there.

"Thank you, ma'am," the stranger said, and swung up on the sorrel's off side. He rode a wide circle back to the wagon, took his Colt from the older man, and slid it into his holster. Then he swung the sorrel straight toward Madeline. Gault's blaze-faced dun was standing at Madeline's left, for Gault had picked up his hat and was in the saddle now.

The stranger drew up on Madeline's right. He lifted his hat again. "You look right pretty now, ma'am," he said. "You're sweet when you aren't doing something you know you hadn't ought to do."

The older man began to talk mule language. The mules dug their necks into their collars, and the wagon began to roll toward them.

Madeline said incredulously, "Are you going on—after this?"

The stranger's gray eyes were like ice, and the pupils touched his upper eyelids as he stared at Gault. His voice came a little queerly, because the sounds were distorted by his bruised and battered lips; but although his face was bloody, and though the blood spots were crusted with dirt, his voice came strong, and she knew with almost fierce exultation that he was a better man than Gault would ever be, a man as immovable as the Caprock itself, once he set out on a course.

"After this there's only one thing can stop me, ma'am, and that's a man who starts throwing lead faster and straighter than me." He went on: "Answerin' your question, ma'am—because I figger when a lady asks a question she's entitled to an answer—this here little sorrel is Indian-broke. She don't like people to mount her on the near side."

He rode off easily, without looking back. The rumbling, creaking wagon passed them, with the black-bearded older man in a shapeless hat working the reins. Madeline and Gault moved toward the creek. He stopped there to wash his face, and she waited silently.

When they reached the cottonwood, her father was watching the wagon follow the Indians' trail up the canyon.

"You can't stop them," he said. "Good or bad, honest or dishonest—when they aim to go, they go. If you stopped this one, there'd be two more to take his place. If the grasshoppers are running them out of the East, we'll see more of them."

Gault said through stiff lips, "The Indians'll take care of him—if he ever gets up there."

Clay Hamilton said, "He looks like a man who can take care of himself."

Wilbarger nodded. "You saw how quick he got rid of his gun so there wouldn't be any excuse for shooting. And you notice how the sorrel was shod with rawhide? That's Apache. That hombre has served time in the Pecos country, and from the looks of things he'd feel perfectly at home ridin' a mama grizzly bear lookin' for her cubs."

Madeline was grateful that they had made no reference to her own part. She looked after the stranger, riding as tall and as strongly as ever on the golden horse with the white mane and tail. He did not now look back; he rode on as if there were no one under the cottonwood, no one else in the entire canyon. He rode on toward the mighty Caprock, and her heart rode with him.

She turned swiftly and went into the ranch house.

CHAPTER 5

WALK FREEMAN, ON THE CALIFORNIA SORREL, WAS tense as he rode past the cottonwood, but he did not look back until they were a mile beyond the Hamilton place. By that time the sun was below the Caprock, and the Yellowhouse canyon was filled with shadows, with

48

here and there the brown or mule-striped dun back of a longhorn steer showing above the gray-green sagebrush. Walk cut a wide circle ahead and came back to the wagon.

"It was right about here the Comanches disappeared," he said. "We can cut their sign in the morning."

Estacado Smith pushed his shapeless hat back on his head. He looked up at the high, forbidding canyon walls. The upper half of the Caprock on their right was yellow in the last light of the sun; the Caprock on their left was now hidden in deep shadow; but both towered far above them, remote, ageless, and seemingly unconquerable. A mouse-colored dirt dauber flew up from the creek, circled them rapidly, and swooped low over the fragrant sagebrush toward the southwest cliff. Estacado followed the bird until it was lost in the shadows, then he looked back up at the Caprock and said in a slow Arkansas drawl, "I don't see no welcome sign nowheres around here."

Walk said dryly, "Didn't you hear the lady tell us to make ourselves at home?"

Estacado fingered his whiskers. "I s'pose the gent that decorated your face was chairman of the Hospitality Committee?"

"Sounds reasonable," said Walk. "Come on, skin these mules across the creek down there and aim for that hackberry tree on the other side. I don't want to be too near the Indians' trail if they should take a notion to come back for an unscheduled conference tonight. Let the mules drink while you're in the water."

Estacado unlimbered his whip and got the mules under way. The iron tires of the wheels struck sparks from the rocks as the wagon lurched across heavy gravel and into the creek. Presently it rose out of the creek on the other side, the wheels dripping water, the mules digging into their collars. Walk had already made a circle ahead. Now he came back. "Head into that cut there. We'll roll up that *arroyada* a ways. There's a wide place in the sand up there for a turnaround, and enough grass on both sides for the stock. We'll sideline the mules and stake Dulce up on the flats. I'll sleep down here by the cut, just in case."

Estacado shook his head lugubriously. "Looks mighty tight in there. No place to run to."

"There's no place to run to anyway," Walk pointed out. "I don't think anybody will bother us, though. These people have got other things to think about. They had a big powwow with the Comanches today, but they didn't get anywhere, because if they had, the Indians would of stayed around to eat."

The wagon crunched up the dry stream bed. Presently Walk called, "Good enough."

The wheels were an inch deep in sand. Estacado swung the two spans of mules and aimed the wagon back toward the Yellowhouse. Walk unsaddled the sorrel, watched her roll on her back, and was satisfied when she went clear over on the third roll. She got up and shook herself and blew the dust out of her nostrils, and he staked her with a horsehair rope.

Estacado unhitched the four mules. He and Walk took them out on a flat and hobbled them. Walk picked out a spot against a bank and looked first for snakes. Then he gathered some driftwood and built a small fire against the bank, fanning the dead cottonwood sticks vigorously with his big hat. They began to blaze with almost no smoke. Estacado got out a large, deep, Dutch-oven-type frying pan and a can of flour. With salt and baking powder he mixed dough in the frying pan while Walk

50

mashed coffee beans on a rock with the butt of his pistol. Estacado looked at him sidewise as if he were about to object, but apparently changed his mind. They worked fast and wasted no words until the frying-pan bread was propped up to face the fire. Walk gathered the mutilated coffee beans on the brim of his hat. Then he took a leather bucket to the stream, and brought back water to hang on the side of the wagon.

Presently Estacado banged the frying pan against a wheel hub and caught the flat, round loaf of bread. He put bacon in the pan and set it on the fire. In a moment or two he tossed the bacon onto a tin plate. Then he banged the frying pan against the wagon wheel to clean it out, half filled it with water, poured the coffee beans into the water, and nested the pan in the coals. They began to eat.

Presently Estacado wiped his mouth with his red bandanna. "That looks like a mighty unhealthy situation down there," he observed.

Walk put his last bit of bread in his mouth. "Maybe not," he said. "I figure it this way. There was eight or ten men there at the tree. That looks like the ranchmen from down the valley were there—especially since we didn't run across any of them all day. The lady came out to turn us back, but I don't think that was official. I think this here red-faced bruiser had something to do with that, but the ranchmen weren't behind it or they would have put in a few hot-lead votes as we went by."

"Was that lady his wife?"

Walk said: "The grease is spread across the water in the frying pan. Reckon the coffee is ready."

Estacado poured coffee into two tin cups.

"Naw," Walk said finally. "She wasn't his wife or he wouldn't of let her go out there alone. You notice he

51

took his time about backing her play." He sighed. "Kind of a relief, too. I'd hate to think of a lady like that married to a wouser like him."

Estacado Smith drained his cup and poured more into it. "I wish you'd pick out a harder rock to mash them coffee beans on," he said, spitting through his beard. "I don't mind a few rock splinters, but that sand that crumbles off of them soft rocks feels so gritty between my teeth."

He poured more for Walk. Then he said, his eyes bright in the depths of his black beard, "I'm willin' to concede she's a neat-lookin' little filly, but do you reckon she's got any cow sense?"

Walk said thoughtfully: "She didn't look so promising today over a short stretch, but I figger there was a lot of things eatin' on her that we didn't know about. I reckon she'd make a good long-horse." He sat up straight and looked downvalley. He took off his hat and looked at it. "She picked up my hat," he said, "and brushed it off." He continued with irrefutable logic, "She didn't pick up *his* hat."

They sat quietly for a few moments, finishing the coffee—more slowly now. A steer bawled shortly up near the northeast wall of the Caprock, made nervous perhaps by kicking out a rattler as it selected a place to lie down. Estacado sat cross-legged, Indian fashion, while Walk sat on his spurs. A cricket sounded down by the creek, and somewhere upstream a bullfrog issued a steady, unanswered call. The night wind swished down from the cliffs and through the bunch grass and the mesquite bushes. The smell of burning wood and the odor of fried bacon and coffee were relaxing. A door slammed down at the Hamilton place, and for a moment a yellow light showed. There was a faint, far-away shudder as horses raced in a big corral, and a squeal as one bit another. Then all was quiet.

Estacado took the frying pan down to the stream and washed it out with gravel. Walk took his bedroll, his saddle, and saddle blanket, and walked down to the cut. He rolled up in the sleeping blanket, wrapped around himself the saddle blanket, strong with horse smell, and went to sleep.

It was still dark when his eyes opened, but downcanyon was a faint streak of gray. Walk sat up, listening. He could hear the bubbling of the water over rocks, but nothing else. Then he heard the wrangler at the Hamilton place come out to the corral and start talking to the night horses. A thin wisp of smoke drifted up from the Hamilton chimney against the widening gray in the southeast. A coyote howled on the southwest rim of the Caprock, and he thought he heard a bobcat scream up near the head of the canyon. The wrangler at the Hamilton place lost his patience and began to talk the kind of language the horses could understand.

Walk rolled to his feet, straightened his black-and-white vest, pulled on his boots and spurs, clamped on his hat, took his gunbelt from under the saddle and buckled it on. His stomach was sore where the big bruiser had kicked him. He went down to the stream and washed his face in the sparkling cold water. It burned in the cuts and bruises, but it left him feeling better.

Half a dozen steers were standing in the stream. Walk went back, picked up his chaps and saddle, and carried them to the wagon.

Estacado was still snoring lustily under the wagon. Walk picked up a handful of sand and dribbled it slowly against the tailboard of the wagon. The snoring stopped instantly. Estacado rolled out between the wheels, wild-eyed. Then he saw Walk, and began to swear. "Some day," he spluttered, "you'll be the cause of my death. Some day a real rattler will sound off, and I won't pay any attention."

"Don't worry," Walk advised. Estacado was already reaching for the frying pan. "That trumpet of yours is enough to clear a quarter section of everything up to and including striped tarantulas."

They wasted no time. Estacado fixed breakfast— bread, bacon, and coffee. Walk brought up the mules and saddled the sorrel. Then he scouted along the creek until he found a short eight-inch cottonwood log, and heaved that on top of the tarpaulin that covered their load. By the time the sun showed a golden edge in the southeast, the wagon was lurching back across the Yellowhouse. They stopped long enough for the stock to drink, and Walk filled a wooden keg with fresh water and lashed it back on the side of the wagon. Then he rode ahead, his gloves slapping from his hip pocket, and picked out the trail of the Comanches up a steep grade; the trail was hardly a foot wide on the side of the cliff. He indicated it to Estacado.

"I can drive up there on my two near wheels," Estacado said calmly, "but who's gonna hold up the right side of the wagon?"

"Why do you think I bought that coil of new rope down in San Antone?" asked Walk. "Now look. This is as far as we can go with the wagon. Drive it over to the left where the canyon wall is straight up and down. Unhitch the mules; we'll load that coil of rope on one and that cottonwood log with the extra wagon stakes and the can of axle grease on another. We'll take the brutes up the trail."

He took a brass-framed .44 Henry carbine from under the wagon seat and put it in a scabbard attached to his saddle horn.

"Say, listen," said Estacado. "You've got 2,500 silver dollars in that wagon. You ain't leavin' that down here."

"Pesos," Walk corrected. "Since the government knocked the skids out from under the silver dollar, I put it all in pesos. More silver in them anyway, and down here they're just as good as gold. But nobody's going to bother that money. I tied it up in a raw hide, and now it's dry and hard as iron. It'd take an ax to break it open."

"Somebody could carry it off."

Walk laughed. "Nobody is gonna carry off a two-hundred-pound rawhide bag on horseback. That money's as safe as we are. Let's get rollin'."

Walk went ahead on the sorrel. Three mules followed him, and then came Estacado on Agathy, the near wheeler, who was a good saddle animal. Half an hour later they were on top, just in time to surprise a grisly-looking lobo wolf escorted by two coyotes fanned out like outriders—all returning to broken country after a night on the Plains. Walk took a quick shot at the lobo, but the wolf was running directly away, and Walk didn't hit him.

Walk picked out a place on the edge of the Caprock to lay the cottonwood log. He fastened the log down, using the wagon stakes as stobs, driving them deep in sod that was hard and dry and firmly packed. He smeared the top of the log with axle grease. Then he paid out a thousand feet of three-quarter-inch new rope over the edge.

Estacado's eyes were bright. "You gonna haul that stuff up on the rope, then take the wagon apart and pull it up too?"

"General idea," Walk said.

Estacado muttered, "Some people is born with brains. Others gets 'em as they goes along." He paused. "I been movin' pretty fast most of *my* life," he said ruefully.

They sidelined three of the mules, still trailing their harness, and Walk and Estacado rode back down the trail. They took off the heavy canvass tarpaulin, folded it in a bundle, and carried it to the base of the cliff. They took the keg of fresh water, and unloaded the wagon. Some of the trade goods was in gunny sacks; some was in boxes or wooden crates. There was a cardboard box filled with small bottles of cheap perfume, a large wooden crate loaded with bright-colored cloth in bolts, a lightly made hogshead filled with pones of bread wrapped in old newspapers, and a box of panocha candy.

There was also an apple box filled with items destined for the ranch Walk intended to have before long: two deep frying pans, a brand new galvanized iron bucket he had bought as a novelty, and tin cups and plates to feed a dozen hands. There was a big iron kettle to be used for making soap, washing clothes, and cooking prairie-dog soup.

There were two grubbing hoes that looked like axes except that the blades were heavier and were turned crosswise at the ends of the handles. Walk and Estacado took these up the canyon a way and cut some mesquite roots.

"There's no wood up on the Plains," Walk said, "except near water—and there isn't much water."

The sharp blades, swung at the end of long handles, were heavy enough to slice through the thick, iron-hard burls if a man put his weight behind them. They gathered two armfuls of roots and went back.

"One o' them grubbing hoes," Estacado observed, "would make a right murderous weapon. You ever see anybody fight with grubbing hoes?"

"No."

"I did once," said Estacado, and paused. "It's all right till somebody gets one of them blades buried crossways in his ribs."

They slid the heavy cowhide filled with pesos out of the wagon; it was stiff and hard as iron, and it took both of them to drag it to the rope. Then they took the wagon apart—wheels, sides, bed, axles, running gear, tongue, and trees. They carried it all to the foot of the cliff. Then they tied the long rope around the heavy tarp, and Walk tied a cross-stick in the rope about twenty feet up.

"You left a couple of hundred feet of rope on this side of the tarp," Estacado observed. "What's that for?"

"There's a shelf that sticks out about halfway up. When the stuff gets to that shelf, you swing it out with your end of the rope till it clears."

He rode the sorrel back up the steep trail. It was midforenoon. He tied the upper end of the long rope to the traces of a mule, and looked over the edge. Five or six hundred feet below, Estacado, leaning back and looking like a pile of dark bush, waved his hat. His cracked voice echoed up from the bottom: "Let 'er go."

Walk picked up the reins and drove the mule straight out onto the plains until the taut rope thumped to announce that the cross-stick had passed over the log. He drove on fifteen feet, then left the mule leaning against the collar and followed the rope back to the log. He pulled the tarp up and over. Then he went for the mule, led it back to the edge, and dropped the rope below again.

It was not fast work, and for the bundle of pesos and the wagon parts he used a second mule up close to wrestle them over the log. By noon a large semicircle on the rim of the Caprock was covered with equipment. Then Estacado and Agathy came up on top. Estacado slid off the mule, waved his hat, and let out a yell. "Son," he said, "you're a genius."

Walk said modestly, "Them's strong words, pardner," but added, with a look around the boxes and bundles and parts accumulated on the prairie, "It does give a man a good feeling, doesn't it?"

"Especially," said Estacado, "when everybody said it couldn't be done."

It was noon, and they were both hungry. Walk had been looking for meat, and had his eye on a prairie-dog town a little way south near the rim. He walked down with the rifle. There were forty or fifty mounds, scattered haphazardly, and there was a sudden concerted scurrying as the prairie-dogs ran to their respective holes, and then at every mound one of the small brown squirrel-like critters sat up on his hind legs and watched. Walk pulled down on one. He thought he hit it, but he never was sure whether they could duck bullets or whether they fell over backward into their holes and kicked themselves down out of reach.

At the shot they all disappeared. He went up and thrust his arm into the hole up to his shoulder, but felt nothing. He went back a hundred yards from the colony and sat down. They began to come out of their holes. He caught one walking across an open space and knocked it end over end. He picked it up and went back to skin it while he waited. Presently he had another, and went to the wagon.

Estacado had the bread cooked. He looked at the dogs

appreciatively but dubiously. "Them things'd be all right if you could get enough of 'em," he said. "They're good eatin'. Only trouble is, they don't stay with you like beef." He began to cut up the small carcasses and lay the pieces in the frying pan. "Meat's scarce this year," he noted.

"Too dry," said Walk, and went on reminiscently, "I got that wagon rod all sharpened up in San Antone to use for a turning spit because I figgered there'd be plenty of buffalo to barbecue, but the only thing we've run into was that young panther down on Double Mountain Fork." He chewed reflectively on a stem of grama grass.

Estacado squinted toward the southwest. "There's been buzzards over that way all morning, and they're spread out. I wonder if somebody's been shootin' buffalo for hides. Maybe that's why the Indians waltzed down in the canyon for a confab."

"Probably," said Walk.

Now they had no water but what was in the wooden keg. They would sling it on the side of the wagon between the two off wheels to keep it out of the sun. Estacado scoured out the frying pan with dirt and brushed out the loose dirt with a handful of grass. Then he stood beside Walk at the rim of the Caprock and looked out over the great valley up which they had come. From where they stood, the Caprock widened out on both sides like the wings of a giant roundup corral, in massive precipices of red, yellow, brown, and purple. At the bottom, between the two Caprocks, stretched the valley to the southeast—a limitless expanse of green and gray, so far below that it seemed like another world, widening out as it led away to the far distance, where it disappeared in a tremendous infinity of blue.

Estacado, leaning backward against the steady push of the wind, took off his hat and stood for a moment, clutching it by the shapeless top. He took a deep breath. "It's like playin' God—bein' up here and lookin' out over all that country," he said in an awed voice.

Walk nodded solemnly. After a moment he turned with a characteristic clipped "Well—!" that sounded like "Welp!"

By midafternoon the wagon had been put together. They hitched up the mules, and Walk saddled the sorrel. He rode up alongside the wagon and looked down into Estacado's whiskery face and grinned. "She's some prairie, isn't she?"

"Flat as a table top," Estacado said emphatically. "It makes them prairies up in Kansas look like mountain country. Some strong wind, too. A man has got to watch his hat."

"They say it blows like this most of the time up here." Walk chuckled. "Nothin' to stop it this side of the Rockies." He leaned on his big Mexican saddle horn with both forearms and stared at the vast sea of grass that stretched endlessly west. He shook his head. "No breaks, no hills, no nothing," he said. "It doesn't even roll. Water would stand flat and soak in wherever it falls. Nothing but prairie and a clear sky and a stiff wind from the west." He looked down. "The grass is burned a little, but it's good grass. Twelve inches high, I reckon. And blue grama grass that'll put tallow on a steer like corn—if it doesn't get burned up."

Estacado shook his head. "I never figgered it was like this."

Walk looked at him curiously. "If you don't know anything about the Llano," he said, "how come they call you Estacado?"

"That's my real name. My mother back in Arkansas said she wouldn't name me by herself; but my pappy was a mountain man, and he warn't never home long enough to decide on a name, so when I was six year old I still didn't have no handle." Estacado looked off across the prairie. "In 1823 my pappy tried to cut across the Plains from New Orleans, lookin' for a short cut to Santa Fe." Estacado fished a plug of Sweet Navy out of his pocket and bit off a chew vigorously, almost angrily. "He found a short cut to hell," he said tersely. "Comanches got him." He slid the plug back into his hip pocket. "My mother said she reckoned that was enough help from him, so she named me Estacado." He wiped his mouth with the back of his hand. "How far do you figger to Mucha Que?" he asked.

Walk moistened his bruised lips with the tip of his tongue. "About seventy-five miles—three more days, I reckon."

"Where do we water next?"

"There's a couple of lakes north of west that I think we can hit sometime tomorrow night if we drive late tonight."

"Trouble is," said Estacado, squinting at the horizon, "there ain't a contaminated thing to go by."

"We'll be following the southern trail that the comancheros used across the Plains for a good many years, coming from New Mexico," Walk said. "It starts up on the Pecos a couple of hundred miles west of here—near Bosque Redondo. I reckon it was used more when Texas was a part of the Spanish Empire." He looked back at the valley below. "There's probably a dozen trails down the Caprock around here, but I don't imagine anybody knows them but the Indians. That's how they can make these surprise raids. The ranchers

61

watch the only trail they know about, but the Indians use a different one."

"What is this here Mucha Que?" asked Estacado.

"Just a place where the traders gather and the Indians bring in their stuff to trade." Walk faced west. "There should be some sort of trail across the Plains, but if there isn't, aim at the setting sun. Well—" The last word was always brisk and curtailed. He straightened up and the sorrel moved. Estacado cracked his whip on the lead mule's rump and began to talk mule. The lead mules pulled out or tried to. The wagon did not move. Estacado swore harder. "Agathy decided to balk," he moaned.

After ten minutes Agathy was still balking. They pushed and pulled and whipped her, and Estacado used his choicest mule language and devised some new expressions, but Agathy ignored them. She sat down in her harness.

"We could build a fire under her," Estacado suggested.

"She'd move out of it and balk as soon as the wagon got over it," Walk said. "Wait a minute. I got an idea." He pulled up a corner of the tarp and dug into the boxes of goods. Presently he came up with a shiny round contraption, and began to work with it. He went by Agathy's head and stood there for a moment, turning a lever. There was a shrill, vibrant ringing. Agathy's eyes shot wide. She lurched into the harness. "Nobody," Walk said, "can ignore one of these here alarm clocks— not even Agathy."

The wagon moved. Walk rode alongside for a while.

"Plenty of good deep grass up here, all right," Estacado called over the creaking of harness and the dry-board noises of the wagon as the iron tires rumbled over the sod. "Sun-cured too—just the way these critters like it."

"It's a little too dry," Walk said. "Some places it's burned. Make a mighty good fire if it ever got started in such a strong wind—and they tell me it blows most of the time."

"You picked out a pretty hostile country to raise cattle in. Why didn't you head for Buffalo Springs up in the north part of the Panhandle?"

Walk watched a terrapin on the ground as they passed; suddenly it pulled in its feet and head and looked like a smooth, gray-brown rock. "Too much Indian trouble up there," he said, "with the buffalo hunters coming across the Cimarron. In a couple of years I s'pose the Indians'll be cleaned out, like everywhere else; but I don't crave to be in the way while that's going on."

"A dry year up here on the prairie would clean a man plumb out," said Estacado.

"Unless," said Walk, ruminating, "a man could find a spring that wasn't taken up. Kit Carson used to talk about a spring—Lost Spring, they always called it."

"Did you know Kit Carson?" asked Estacado, with awe in his voice.

Walk Freeman laughed. "Some," he said.

"What about Lost Spring?" Estacado asked, after digesting this.

"The story is that there was a good spring somewhere in the central region of the Llano, but that in 1841, while the Texian-Santa Fe expedition was camped at the east foot of the plains, the Comanches, believing then that the white man would try to freeze them out, partially plugged up the big spring with boulders. Now it's supposed to look like any other small spring, and its water dribbles down the stream bed a few miles and then either dries into the ground or evaporates. They claim old Ossakeep, the Comanche chief, did that so the country wouldn't look good to the whites. He always did figure the whites wouldn't be happy until they took over the Llano," Walk said soberly. "Maybe that's why the Comanches hate Texians so much. Reckon you can't blame them."

Walk rode around behind the wagon and up on the other side to examine the lashings of the water keg. When he came up even with Estacado again, he said: "I don't quite figure one thing. That little lady was right vehement about us comin' up here to trade. I know the comancheros don't claim to be the cream of society, but they been trading across the Plains for nearly a hundred years; they ought to have *some* rights. I don't figger that is exactly what was eatin' on her; she acted like we was a couple of Gila monsters with the plague."

Estacado looked up at him quizzically. "Ain't we?"

"By no means," Walk said elegantly. "We're traders. I got $300 worth of honest trade goods in this here outfit. I come up here because 2,500 silver pesos won't go very far toward starting a ranch, but I figger I can make $300 go as far as $3,000, the way they trade up here, and then I'll have a herd and 2,500 pesos to operate on. That way I can get about ten years' head start. No, sir," he said emphatically, "I come up here to do a legitimate and time-honored business, and I aim to do it. This stuff in the wagon has got to be moved, and we've got to find a spot up here for an outfit."

"You brought all that money along with you," Estacado observed. "You got ev'rything in one basket. If Indians or outlaws set in this game, you'll lose the whole works. Why didn't you wait a couple of years till things get more settled up here?"

"Next year or year after," Walk said, "the Indians will be gone, and the trade stuff won't do any good—and by that time all the grassland will be taken up too." He added, "Opportunity is for those who knock."

"What about the brands on this stuff you're goin' to trade for?"

Walk hesitated. "The comancheros mostly trail it west and northwest. Over in New Mexico Territory they aren't too fussy about brands. Anyhow, I figure on keeping my stuff, and by the time the owners get around to claiming it—if it has been stolen—there'll be plenty of young stuff carrying my brand."

"Ain't that just a wee mite dishonest?"

Walk said fiercely, "Is it any more dishonest than watchin' the carpetbagger courts turn your stuff over to trail drivers that never come back with your money?"

Estacado looked straight ahead at the lead mule's ears. "That don't make it right."

Walk took a deep breath. "I spent four years in the war," he said. "That was wasted. I spent six years trying to get somewhere under carpetbagger rule. That was wasted. I spent two years with the Apaches. That makes twelve years. Now it's time for me to make some money and make it quick. I'm thirty-two. Why should I start in from scratch?"

"You ain't exactly startin' that way," Estacado pointed out. "You got this outfit and 2,500 pesos."

"I'd have ten times that much if it wasn't for the war," Walk said stubbornly.

"Maybe you *can* git rich in a hurry by not lookin' too close at brands," Estacado said, "but somehow it don't seem to suit you."

Walk looked at the far horizon of unlimited grass.

65

"It's not all stolen stock," he said slowly. "Just because an Indian has it is no sign he stole it."

"I ain't ever heard of no big Indian herds up here."

Walk frowned a little, but he said stubbornly: "We're gonna trade this stuff to the Indians and come out of the deal with a herd of cows and enough horses to start a ranch. Then we're going to find Lost Spring, unplug, and let 'er roll. We'll have the finest little ranch on the Llano."

Estacado reminded him sourly, "Providin' the Comanches don't buy in."

"I'm not killin' any buffalo for hides," Walk pointed out sharply.

Estacado said morosely, "I hope the Comanches remember that when they start swingin' them scalping knives."

Presently Walk said in a quiter tone: "There's only one thing bothering me right now. What part does that big bruiser play in all this?" Walk rubbed his stomach tenderly. "His chaps didn't carry any Tres Casas brand," he observed.

"Smelt like polecat to me," said Estacado, tightening his nose. "And that brown-haired lady: she's got a nice face, and she's built like yearlin' heifer that's been on deep grass all summer—but she's a vixen, son. She's a vixen."

Walk stood up in his stirrups and looked back. "I'll find out more about that," he said, "when I get my herd started and find a place for a ranch up here."

Estacado lowered his eyes. He swung his arm and his long whip snaked out over the lead mule's head and made a sound like the crack of a pistol. The mule veered to the left.

Walk shouted dryly, "Keep 'em headed into the

66

setting sun—or can't you skin more than one span of mules at a time?"

That evening Walk made a change in their equipment. He unfastened the rawhide hobbles from the sorrel's neck and threw them away, and had Estacado do the same with the mules. "We can use gunny sacks," he said. "Rawhide hobbles on a horse's neck mean a Texian—and Comanches hate Texians."

"The New Mexicans don't like us neither," Estacado observed.

"Not too much," said Walk. "They say a Texian shoots off his mouth too much." He chuckled. "But I reckon what really riles 'em is that Texians go out on a limb and claim they can do anything; and then when the Mexicans make fun of 'em, it gets their dander up and they go ahead and do it. Anyway, the Mexicans haven't had much use for us since the Alamo."

Estacado said thoughtfully, "We ain't got many friends around here, have we?"

CHAPTER 6

FOR THREE DAYS THEY ADVANCED ACROSS THE endless prairies. Walk had seen many prairies; there were prairies in Kansas and prairies west of the Cross Timbers, but this was the daddy of them all: a sea of gray and green, stretching level and flat on every side, unbroken even by a tree.

It makes a man feel kinda little," Estacado observed after two days of endless horizons. "And it makes him feel kinda big too, to be a part of somthin' so almighty whoppin' big."

"It's the only place I ever traveled," Walk said

presently, "where the horizon goes right along ahead of you. Other places you ride a while, and hills or mountains or something come along from time to time. You see them in the far distance, and after while you catch up to them or go past them; but out here you go and go and go, and there's still just as much ahead as there ever was—and more behind."

"If there'd only be a tree once in a while," said Estacado wistfully.

But there wasn't. There wasn't even mesquite out on the prairie, and there was no prickly-pear cactus. Occasionally there would be a small clump, about grass-high, of gray-green bear grass or Spanish dagger, with its stiff, slender, blade-shaped leaves that grew up and outward from a common center on the ground in a thick, forbidding cluster, with the leaf ends needle-shaped and very sharp; usually the clusters carried a tall spike of large white blossoms straight up from the center.

They found the lake the second night, but it was low and salty, and they used the water cautiously. "There's not even much mesquite around it," Walk said the next morning as they harnessed the mules. "I reckon it's dry most of the time." He snapped the breast straps into the end of the wagon tongue.

"Why ain't there any mesquite up on the Plains?" asked Estacado.

Walk said thoughtfully, "Well, it's like this: mesquite beans have such a hard shell they don't sprout unless they go through an animal's digestive system."

"Fussy, ain't they?" Estacado observed dryly.

Walk went on, unperturbed. "Wild horses are the only animals that eat the beans to amount to anything—and they don't go far from water."

Presently Estacado observed, "I don't know how

68

anything ever gets a chance to take root up here, the way the wind blows."

Walk nodded. "You notice how she changes sometimes.? There'll be a few minutes' lull, and all of a sudden she'll start comin' in from the south or southwest, and blow like that for hours. Then she may change back again."

It was Estacado who pointed out that there was a full moon that night and that there would be plenty of trading in the next week or two.

There was an occasional buffalo wallow—a shallow, saucerlike depression, the bottom of which would be covered with caked mud crisscrossed by drying-cracks and sun-baked until it resembled black jelly. And twice they passed mounds of earth with little or no grass growing on them. One occurred in the middle of a prairie-dog town. They puzzled Walk. "Looks like a grave," he said, "only it isn't quite big enough. What do you figger?"

"You got me," said Estacado. "There's nothing valuable buried there or they'd have hidden it better."

None of those things stood up above the level plain of grass, and none were seen until a man was upon them.

It was the early afternoon of the third day when Walk, scouting ahead, made a circle and came back to the wagon. "Something on the horizon up ahead," he said. "Looks like a row of wagons in a mirage."

Estacado dug out his ear with his left third finger and snapped the dry dirt to the ground. "I ain't seen a hill *or* a cloud since we got up on the Llano," he said, and added hopelessly, "It's prob'ly the end of the world."

"Maybe not. Anyway, there's a shallow draw starts up there about a quarter of a mile. Follow that up on the left side. Looks as if there's water in it sometimes."

Estacado snorted. "I could spit a bigger stream than anything up here."

They jumped a herd of sixteen antelope along the draw; the animals bounced up and seemed to float away far out of reach, their white rumps shining in the sun.

Late in the afternoon Walk leaned back in the saddle. and said, "There's a hill, all right, and there are wagons this side of it. It's close, too—just over that long rise. I reckon we're hitting Mucha Que on the nose."

Estacado was thoughtful. "I wonder," he said, "if they're gonna like us newcomers for buttin' in on their spread."

But Walk was cantering ahead. He had seen movement in the draw. He circled out a little and pulled in cautiously. Estacado saw the movement and reached for the rifle under the seat; he laid it across his lap. The mules pulled on steadily, the wagon creaking and groaning in a way that was much like breathing, for it seemed to have a regular rhythm.

The California sorrel had frozen, watching the draw, ears cocked forward. Walk Freeman's brown right hand rested lightly on the butt of his Walker. He did not expect anything dangerous, but the Colt was the only law on the Llano, and it was well to be legally prepared.

The top of a head of black hair rose above the grass to the left of where he was watching. It startled him. He saw a part down the center of the head and two tightly braided glossy black strands, one on each side. The head moved to the left and away, rising gradually higher, and Walk realized the Indian was walking slowly and apparently laboriously up a small swale that led away from the draw and toward the camp that was now out of sight over the rise, but probably not far away.

"Holy Christopher!" Estacado said, half under his

breath. The Indian looked around, and then Walk saw what Estacado Smith, in his riper wisdom, had discerned first. The Indian was a girl. She wasn't dumpy, as were most of the Comanche women at an early age, but slim and straight, with breasts swelling her buckskin jacket. She had heard Estacado's exclamation, and looked back. She wasn't over twenty, with finely bronzed skin, straight nose, red lips, and black, questioning eyes.

Estacado cracked his whip over the mules. "Wait'll I git thar! I'll talk sign language to her. These Indians don't never talk Spanish, especially a squaw."

Walk grinned back at him and moved the sorrel toward the girl. She was up on the level now, and he saw she was carrying a huge wooden pail of water. She stood there watching him, holding the pail in front of her with both hands. Estacado was swearing at the mules in Texas English, and the wagon was rumbling up. Walk lifted his hat, said, *"Buenos días, señorita,"* dropped his hat back on his head, and with that arm swept up the big pail from her hands. *"Perdóneme,"* he said.

She smiled and said in soft, liquid Spanish, *"Le doy las gracias más espresivas por el favor que me hace, señor."*

Walk stopped the sorrel on her haunches and looked at Estacado, who was up with them. "I thought you said the lady didn't talk Spanish," he said dryly.

The girl's voice arose before Estacado could sputter out his first word. It was a nice clear voice, and it said in very slightly but delightfully accented American, "I speak English too, sir." She gave Estacado a sidewise, quizzical smile.

Estacado stared at her. He looked at the mules on

71

which he had been heaping profanity. Then he looked back at the girl, and burst out, "You musta had a damn' good education, ma'am."

Walk said, "Where you takin' this water?"

"To the camp." She gestured with a well shaped brown arm.

Walk started the sorrel, holding the pail carefully to avoid spilling the water. The girl walked alongside. Walk watched her from the corner of his eye. "What's your name?" he asked.

"They have call' me Quita," she said.

"Nice name," Walk said. He was listening to Estacado trying to skin the mules with a minimum of profanity. It was doubly amusing because Estacado didn't like Indians, and pretended to look down on them—particularly on Indian women. This, in view of the fact that the only time a hard-shell Westerner tried to refrain from profanity was in the presence of those he considered ladies, was indicative of Estacado's reaction toward Quita.

She had clean, well shaped lines, like a filly with good breeding, and there was pride in the way she held her head, and grace in the lightness of her step.

They went over the top of the rise, and Walk stopped for a moment. The sun had just gone out of sight behind a low red-dirt cliff a quarter of a mile straight in front of them. Extending toward them from the cliff was an irregular double row of animal-drawn vehicles: a couple of prairie freighters like Walk's, an old Conestoga with billowing top, a flat farmer's wagon, and many carretas—big two-wheeled Mexican carts with wheels sawed from sections of large cottonwood trees. All were unhitched, and they faced one another across a rough "street" of grass that had been pretty well trodden down.

To the north and around at the foot of the cliff was an Indian village of half a dozen buffalo-hide tepees and the usual litter of small, smokeless fires with squaws sitting around them, Indian babies on blankets, small naked children chasing each other, and Indian saddles tossed at the base of every tepee. "Cheyennes," Walk said slowly.

Quita nodded. "They have been here trading. They leave tomorrow to go north to get the whisky Ramón has promised them."

"How far north?"

"Maybe ten, twenty miles."

"Why?" asked Walk.

"If he gives them the whisky now, they drink it, then they steal all the horses and cows, and want to trade again. But if they are far away, they look for other Indians to fight. That is smart, no?"

Walk nodded. "It looks like trading with the Indians is more complicated than I figgered," he observed, and stood up in his stirrups. "What kind of a celebration they havin' up there back of the wagons?" he asked.

Quita looked sober. "Is a fight," she said. "Ramón is fighting *el señor* Pegleg." She stumbled over the last word.

Walk stared at her. "Pegleg? You mean a man with a wooden leg?"

"He has a—how you say?—post for a leg."

Estacado had drawn up behind them. "You reckon that's Pegleg Popham?" he called to Walk. "He said he was headed this way when we saw him in San Antone."

Walk nodded, looking absently at Quita. "He wanted to come out here and get a stake so he could settle down. I reckon frontier life got to be a little rough for him after the Mescaleros burned off his foot." He

73

looked toward the tight group, heard a rapid thudding of feet and the sharp crack of a hard blow. "You reckon he needs some help?" he asked Estacado.

"Pegleg's an old Indian fighter," Estacado pointed out. "He can take care of himself. Anyway, we come up here to do some business—not to settle other people's fights."

Walk grunted and rode on. They drew up to the street of vehicles, and Walk gave the big wooden pail back to the girl. To his surprise she did not cut across to the Indian camp, but carried it to the first big wagon and hung it from the tailboard.

"Whatta you think?" asked Estacado.

Walk was watching the knot of men—Indians, Mexicans, whites. He heard a moment or two of grunting as the two men strained at each other, then a heavy thud as one was hurled to the ground, followed by a rush of feet, and low, muttered oaths. The crowd gave and moved with the fighters, but it never thinned, and no one seemed to look toward the new wagon. Walk could not distinguish the men in the center, but he knew from the harsh, uncontrolled breathing that the men had been at it for some time.

"Injun fightin'," muttered Estacado.

Walk nodded. These were rough men in a lawless country, and they meant to kill any way they could.

Estacado said, "Reckon we might as well pull in and get set."

Walk nodded. He turned his face from the fight and said: "Pull in by this big wagon. Looks like a good spot to me."

But Quita was at his side immediately. She said, "*No, señor,*" in a low voice. She was shaking her head vigorously. "You must go to that end." She pointed

74

toward the cliff.

Walk looked at her, and saw the genuine anxiety in her face. He took a deep breath. "O.K.," he said to Estacado. "Skin those mules down to the other end. I got a hunch she's talkin' straight." He looked toward the group around the fight. "If so, it's their game and we're takin' a hand. I reckon we better play their rules for a while."

They drove into position beside a two-wheeled cart. Their wagon was now the last in line. The low red cliff was fifty yards away on the west; to the south was flat prairie; to the north the mesquite bushes were thick between them and the draw, and grew taller toward the draw.

No person paid any attention to them, and they saw no one along the street. Walk unsaddled the sorrel. Estacado muttered as they unhitched the mules: "It don't look like a healthy spread to me, Walk. When they do sashay our way, they may look at us awful hard."

Presently they had the harness hung on the sides of the wagon. Estacado mounted Agathy and rode off to the south, leading the sorrel and the other mules, to look for pasture.

Walk didn't like the looks of things either. He walked up the street of wagons. Quita was boiling water in a big pot over a fire of glowing buffalo chips. Walk looked at the knot of men. "They're still fighting," he said.

Quita looked up briefly. "*Sí*. Ramón's fights last a long time," she said casually,

Walk leaned against the wheel of the wagon. "Who's Ramón?" he asked.

She looked up, wide-eyed. "Ramón ees—how you say?—*capitán*—boss. Everybody has fear of Ramón," she said matter-of-factly.

Walk grinned. "I don't imagine *everybody* is afraid of Ramón. You ever heard the poem about the fleas?"

Her eyes were wide and softly brown, like an antelope's. "No, *señor.*"

He recited gravely, watching her face: "Big fleas have little fleas upon their backs to bite 'em; little fleas have smaller fleas, and so on *ad infinitem.*"

She was lost. She shook her head slowly. "*Qué dice eso, señor?*"

"It means," he said gently, "that no matter how big a coyote grows, he always quits howling when a lobo wolf goes by."

She asked thoughtfully, "You speak of Ramón?"

"Sure," he said carelessly. "I'd mighty near bet my bat there's somebody bigger than him on the other side of the corral."

Her eyes lighted up. Her answer set him back on his heels. "Oh, *sí*! Yes, there is the *beeg* boss. He is more to be feared than Ramón."

He asked, "Who's the big boss?"

Her eyes dropped. She shrugged her straight shoulders, making a lovely movement under the soft buckskin of her jacket. "*Es hombre,*" she said. "*Yo no sé como se llama.* He is a man. I don't know his name."

He looked at her a moment. She did not raise her eyes, and he knew it would be useless to ask more. She had started talking Spanish, and he knew the next answer would be the ungrammatical "*No sabe.*" He straightened. He lifted his gun belt and settled it on his hips. Then he turned and walked stiff-legged to the group of men watching the fight in the twilight. It was time to take a look at Ramón.

CHAPTER 7

WALK WAS HALF A HEAD TALLER THAN MOST OF THOSE around the fight, and they gave way as he slowly pushed through. There were short, powerfully built Comanches with braided hair and a characteristic odor of decayed meat; there were taller Cheyennes. There were swarthy Mexicans in black trousers, red sashes, and tall straw hats with turned-up brims. There were bearded, sun-burned whites in dirty buckskins and moccasins, and coonskin or squirrel caps. The Comanches had powerful hunting bows slung over their shoulders; the Mexicans had knives in their sashes, and some had heavily loaded gun belts; the whites had pistols, and some carried long-barreled breech-loading rifles. The Comanches looked at Walk's tall hat, and he sensed their instant animosity, for the Comanches did not like anything that suggested Texas.

The Cheyennes looked at him without particular feeling. The Mexicans glared at him with wide, suspicious, belligerent black eyes, and fingered the knives at their sashes. The whites watched him from narrowed eyes, with sun-baked lips held thin, and some twisting of position to get gun hands in the clear. These things he noted as he went through, and though he was not contemptuous of them, he pushed on until he could look over the front row of men that surrounded the fighting area.

One of the men was Pegleg Popham, and he was holding his own. In spite of the connotation of his name, he was no older than Walk, but he had been using his wooden leg for a long time and had learned how to fight with it. He stood on it now, in the center of the circle,

77

and spun on it as Ramón tried to get behind him. Popham was a leather-faced man with deep lines that hardly belonged in the face of one his age; he was tall and lithe, and though he was breathing heavily he did not seem to be tired. The wooden stob that served as his right lower leg was about eight inches long, and he had full use of that knee. Walk was glad Popham had learned to take care of himself, but it was Ramón he had come to see. Walk's eyes narrowed as he watched.

Ramón, who was trying to circle Popham, was a heavily built man but quick on his feet, like a longhorn cow. He was halfbreed, Walk thought, with the features of a white but the coloring of a Mexican. He wore a green silk sash around his waist. He was not breathing any harder than Pegleg. His eyes were black and glittery, like the eyes of a rattler; his lips were drawn back, and large white teeth gleamed in his brown face. Straight black hair stuck to his sweating forehead, and the handle of a big bowie knife protruded from the green sash; below the sash was a tuft of black hair that signified the knife was carried in a sheath made from the tail of a buffalo calf.

Ramón darted to one side. Pegleg spun on his wooden leg. Ramón reversed and shot back, but Pegleg crossed him up by continuing on around. He met Ramón coming in. His right leg flashed and the wooden peg sank into Ramón's belly. Ramón grunted but seemed to absorb the blow. His big arms clutched at Pegleg, but the one-legged man hopped backward and out of range with astonishing agility. Ramón stepped back to get his balance. The men moved and left Pegleg in the center.

Ramón began to circle again. Walk saw that he was taking his time, perhaps to tire Pegleg, or perhaps more to enjoy the final kill, for there seemed to be no doubt in

Ramón's mind of the outcome. Walk did not quite understand that, for Pegleg, with his height and his toughness and his unusual ability in use of the wooden leg, looked formidable. Then Ramón darted in straight. Pegleg met him with the wood, but Ramón sidestepped with the grace of a bullfighter and then, catching Pegleg off balance, pushed on the man's chest with both big hands. Pegleg went down hard on his back. Ramón did not follow up.

The watching Indians grunted; most of the comanchero traders were silent, though some laughed shortly.

Pegleg rolled on the ground and bounced up. This time he had a big jackknife in his hand, with the blade open. Walk drew in his breath. Pegleg was tiring and had decided to risk a knife fight. That meant he was desperate, for Ramón's bowie knife, with its sharp foot-long blade, was far more deadly than the jackknife. Walk felt Estacado slide into place at his left. At Walk's right, a small, grizzled Mexican with deep-set eyes was fingering a loop in a horsehair rope.

Pegleg attacked. He went in slashing. Ramón tried to wrestle with him, but when Pegleg backed away the semblance of a grin was no longer on Ramón's face. His neck on the left side was bloody where Pegleg had gone for the jugular but missed. The bowie knife was in Ramón's hand, its long, narrow, slightly curved blade forward, the edge up. He held it low, pointed at Pegleg's abdomen. His white teeth gleamed in the gathering darkness, and his eyes were those of a snake striking.

But Pegleg came in again, careful, deadly, fast, moving with a curious twisting pivot on his wooden leg. When he backed away, Ramón was breathing hard, and the left shoulder of his shirt was wet with blood. Pegleg

79

had a small gash on the outer side of his left forearm, but he paid no attention to it. He had Ramón on the defensive, and he attacked.

Ramón sidestepped and was at Pegleg's back. He lunged at Pegleg's kidneys with the big knife, but Pegleg recovered his balance and whirled. His back was almost in front of Walk. Ramón backed away, and Walk saw him shoot a glance at somebody over Pegleg's shoulder. Pegleg started forward. Then, inexplicably, he floundered. He almost fell on his face, but struggled frantically to get his balance. While he was doing that, Ramón carved out his intestines with the bowie knife. Pegleg gathered himself enough to crash his wooden leg into Ramón's face before he went down.

Walk's jaws were grimly clamped together. Ramón stood over Pegleg, waiting for him to try to get up, but Popham was a dead man. He died cursing Ramón.

Ramón ostentatiously wiped the blood from the long blade of his knife with the ends of the green sash. Then he drew a deep breath. The malevolent grin came back on his brown face. He put the knife back in the calf-tail sheath. Then he looked around at the silent audience. "You saw," he said. "This carrion forced a fight on me. You saw that?"

Some nodded slowly, watching him.

"You saw me whip him in a fair fight—yes?"

The Indians grunted. Somebody said "Yes" gutturally, and the crowd began to break up. But Walk Freeman, with Estacado trying to hold him back with his gnarled fingers on Walk's left arm, stepped out from the crowd. "I don't gener'ly make a practice of mixing in other people's fights," he said. "I'm willin' to admit I was tempted on account of the other gent's being a one-legged man, but I didn't see the start of the fight and I

80

didn't figure it was any of my affair." He looked straight into Ramón's black eyes. "I was ridin' my temper with a tight rein until you asked me to testify." A circle began to open around him. "If I keep my mouth shut now, it's the same as me saying you killed him in a fair fight. And that isn't so," he said levelly. "You had help from the grandstand. The one-legged man was murdered." He watched Ramón, and waited for his answer.

Ramón was obviously startled at opposition, but he became alert at Walk's last word. His black eyes swept over Walk, and he said, with a half snarl, "The coyotes drag up a lot of pilgrims today—no?"

"No," Walk said coldly. "The coyotes walk around with the men. I'm no pilgrim," he warned. "Don't count on it." He took a deep breath, and added, "I saw your signal, and I saw your side-kick pull up a loop on Popham's wooden leg."

Ramón glared at him. "You no like that fight, huh?"

"I like the one I'm gonna have better," said Walk.

Ramón looked him up and down. Craftiness came in his brown face. "You're *tejano*," he said. "You don't fight with the hands—no? You fight with the peestol."

Walk said coldly, "I fight with the pistol—yes. I fight with the knife—yes. I fight with the hands—yes. You're tired. I fight the way you choose—*mister*," he said scornfully.

Ramón swelled up. But he was cautious. "Throw away your peestol," he said in a harsh voice. "You weel die slow."

Walk turned to Estacado. Estacado shook his bushy head, but he extracted the pistol from Walk's holster. Walk faced Ramón. "I will die hard," he said, and launched a fist at the half-breed.

81

It connected a little above the green sash. Ramón grunted and closed. He tried to throw Walk off his feet, but Walk stepped back and swung at him, his long arms pumping, his fists sinking into Ramón's midsection.

The circle was solid around them. Ramón's breath began to whistle through his white teeth. He launched a heavy kick at Walk's groin, but Walk saw it coming in the semi-darkness. He moved back a step and brought up one foot under Ramón's outstretched leg. Ramón fell heavily. Walk watched him get up.

He ran at Walk, head down, suddenly, like a proddy cow with a new calf. He hit Walk in the abdomen, and knocked him flat. Walk tried to roll, but Ramón straddled him and battered him in the face. Walk brought up his long legs. He kicked at the small of Ramón's back with the hard toe of his boots, and the man grunted. Walk started a second swing, and saw the dull flash of the knife aimed at the hollow in his collarbone. But a shot over his head deafened him. There was a blast of yellow fire, and he felt stinging hot particles of powder on his face. He heard the ring of a bullet on the knife, and saw Ramón holding his hand as if it were paralyzed. Walk threw him off, almost smothered in the powder smoke. He got to his feet and charged, beating the man back with full-bodied blows in the face. Ramón's right hand came back into use, but too late. Walk gave him one last crashing pair of right and left blows, and the man went down. Walk waited. Ramón raised himself on one elbow. Then he sank back down.

Walk turned to Estacado and took his pistol. "Nice shootin'," he said. He grinned and added, "—through all them whiskers."

He chucked the pistol in its holster, looked around

and asked quietly, "This here was a private fight, wasn't it?"

The little Mexican in the tall straw hat with the turned-up brim, who had used the *mecate* on Popham, said in a high voice: "You cannot beat Ramón! He weel keel you dead."

"Some other time," said Walk.

The little Mexican seemed about to say more, but under Walk's steady gaze he did not. But a grizzled, old, short-bearded comanchero in a coonskin cap with the tail hanging down his back, said testily: "I don't like the way you're settin' in the saddle, stranger. Air you the law?"

"I'm no law," said Walk. "I'm a trader. I come up here to do some business with the Indians. I understand it's open."

"You got a license from the Army?"

"Yes," said Walk. "Want to see it?"

"If I did," the old man said, "it would be the first one I seen up here on the Plains." There was dead silence for a moment.

"Next thing we know," said a long, loose-jawed man, "you'll be callin' in the Army to protect your rights."

"Don't you figger," Walk asked softly, "that I can take care of my own?"

There was no answer to that. Then the slack-jawed man said truculently, "We got our rules here, and we enforce 'em ourselves. This here pegleg gent figgered he could stash his wagon at the front end of the line, and he got what was comin'."

Walk paused a moment, and swallowed hard. He said finally, "If they're good rules, I'll go by them as long as I know what they are."

There was muttering, but the men drifted away. Walk

and Estacado went back to their spot near the cliff. Walk looked on the ground for snakes. They spread a small tarp under the wagon, and laid their blankets on it. Then they sat with their backs against the front wheel, watching the way they had come. There was yelling down at the open end, and considerable activity. Presently a wagon burst into flames. It was dry, and burned fiercely, the yellow flames reaching high and lighting up the entire street. The light showed gunny sacks, boxes filled with goods, and a small keg scattered around the fire. Walk's lips were tight. The straw-hatted Diego came loping out of the dark on horseback, dragging Pegleg's body by a lariat. He disappeared in the darkness to the east.

When the fire had burned down to coals, Ramón appeared, his face discolored in spots, wearing a big, square-topped black hat of shaggy, plush-like material, with buckskin thongs tied under his chin. In the light of the burning wagon he began to divide the goods on the ground. The traders stepped up as he called their names, and took armfuls of goods and carried them to their own wagons.

Before the fire died down, Diego came loping back into camp.

"He didn't have time to bury him," Estacado commented.

"The buzzards'll take care of the carcass tomorrow," Walk said thinly.

"Right nice mess o' pirates *we* picked out," Estacado commented sourly. "They leave that spot up there wide open for pilgrims, and when somebody does fall into it, then Ramón cuts him up and they divide the feller's goods."

Walk spoke through a throat so tightly constricted by

the cold-bloodedness of what he had seen that his words were painful. "It's no wonder this bunch of comancheros don't set so well with decent folks," he said. "A lowdown, double-distilled, calf-killin' lobo wolf *net* is a respectable citizen compared to these gents here."

Estacado nodded solemnly. "This camp," he said, "is really organized—and that feller Ramón is the head executioner."

CHAPTER 8

EARLY IN THE MORNING WALK GOT A GRUBBING HOE out of the wagon, gathered an armful of small loose brush and cut a few knots of gnarled mesquite root. Estacado had brought in a pile of dried buffalo chips on his way back from setting out the stock the night before. He built a fire.

"Not much stock around here this summer, it looks like," said Estacado, mixing dough.

"Too much pressure from the government people," said Walk.

"But there'll be stock." He added thoughtfully, "I reckon we better shy away from anything with Yellowhouse canyon brands."

Estacado did not answer.

"We can pasture the ridin' stock north of the draw," he said.

They cooked in the shade of the wagon on the side next to the red cliff, which in the glare of the hot morning sun seemed hardly higher than a tall man's head. Up and down the street, men were cooking and eating. The loose-jawed man sat under the front end of his wagon licking his fingers. The grizzled Mexican in the big straw hat with the upturned brim—Diego— saddled up a grullo and rode off to the north. Ramón leaned against the front of his wagon, with one foot propped up on the wagon tongue, eating a thick slab of buffalo meat in his fingers. He wore the tight black pants of the Mexican, the green silk sash, and the shaggy, square-topped black hat. He was talking to the shortbearded man in the coonskin cap.

"The gent lickin' his fingers is Batty Simpkins," said Estacado in a low voice. "They got a rope waitin' fer him down at San Saba. Seems like somebody stole a bunch of hosses one night and killed the owner." Estacado knocked the bread out of the pan against the hub of the wagon wheel, put the pan on the coals, set a slab of bacon on the top of the water keg, and carved off a thick, greasy slice with a jackknife. "Seems like somebody got the notion Batty was a little too quick with his gun that night," Estacado went on. "They been lookin' fer him ever since. And the gent in the coon cap is named Bear Hug Hobart. Don't give a damn fer nothin'. Roped a grizzly bear once and brung him in alive." He dropped bacon in the pan. "Him and I scouted for Colonel Ford against the Comanches at Antelope Hills in 1868, and the colonel give him a black mark fer lootin' when he shoulda been scoutin'. They say he warn't particular who he looted, either."

Walk broke the pan bread in half and bit a piece out of one half. He chewed slowly for a moment. "I reckon there's more refined places than Mucha Que," he conceded.

"Why don't we sashay on west and trade with the Mexicans?" asked Estacado.

Walk smiled. "Our stuff," he said, "doesn't exactly

appeal to Mexicans. They might like the beads and the calico, but have you got any idea what they'd do with four dozen alarm clocks?"

"Well," Estacado said judiciously, "I'm willin' to face the real facts. Them people wouldn't use no alarm clock to get up by—and I don't say I exactly blame 'em. Some people call 'em lazy, but maybe they just know how to live better'n we do."

"Besides," Walk said thoughtfully, "the governor of New Mexico Territory has issued a proclamation against the comancheros, and the Army is supposed to be enforcing it." He looked to the west. "I reckon it's only fifteen or twenty miles to the New Mexico line from here, and that's as close as we better go." With his jackknife he speared a piece of bacon from the pan that Estacado lifted off the coals. He watched the grease drip from it. "I come out here," he said, unexpectedly defensive even to himself, "because I figgered I could get a new start quicker this way. I still figger it."

Estacado looked around the end of the wagon toward Ramón. "Just the same," he said, "look out for that 'breed. He looks fat, but it's mostly muscle. Them kind fool you. He didn't get to be boss of this bunch of hyenas for nothin'."

Estacado poured water in the pan for coffee. Most of the comancheros had finished their breakfast and now were beginning to circulate up and down the street, but none came near Walk's wagon. He and Estacado drank their coffee in silence. The sun was high over the unbroken prairie to the east, and it was hot enough to sap the strength from man or beast.

Estacado said: "The Comanche moon will be in full swing tonight. You reckon they're raidin' down along the Yellowhouse?"

"If they do," Walk said, "I hope that big bruiser in the red calfskin vest works off some of his meanness on 'em." He changed subjects thoughtfully. "Did you notice that Indian girl chewin' on a bacon rind while Ramón ate buffalo?"

"I notice it ain't hurt her figger none," said Estacado. He looked at Walk from under bushy eyebrows. "You ain't accepted much of my advice," he said, "but you better take a long look at your hole card before you go shining up to Quita. I don't know what she is to Ramón, but she belongs to his wagon. That's plain enough." He finished his coffee and went to look after the mules and the sorrel.

Walk took the frying pan and a water bucket. He was startled to see the street deserted by the time he reached the front of his wagon, but he walked the length of the street and turned to the draw.

The draw at its deepest was about six feet below the level of the grass on the prairie, and it was spotted with mesquite bushes that offered thin shade, but over the cracked squares of sunbaked mud the buzzing blueflies were so thick a man could not have lain down to rest.

He was surprised but not displeased to see Quita sitting on the bank a little way below the path, with her bare feet in the running water. Her buckskin skirt was decorously wrapped around her legs below her knees, and she held it there with one slim bronze hand while she looked up at him.

"*Cómo sé llama V.?*" she asked.

"Walk," he said. "Walk Freeman." He turned the bucket on its side and slowly submerged it in the water to avoid stirring up mud.

She frowned very neatly. "Walk?" she repeated.

"Yes. *Anda—ándale*—Walk." He lifted the bucket.

88

"Why did everybody fall back into their holes when I walked down the street just now?" he asked. "It looked like a prairie-dog town."

"Maybe," she said, "it is because you are a very strong fighter—*muy fuerte,*" she said with vigor. "Or *tal vez*—perhaps—it is because you are *tejano*. Or perhaps they do not trust you."

"Trust me?" He had half turned to go back. Now he stopped.

"Maybe," she said, watching him, "you are a spy for the Army—no?"

"No," he said. "Definitely no. I'm working for nobody but Walk Freeman. I hope I can cinch that before somebody gets killed."

"Me too," she said, and slanted her head to one side. "You are so *chico* so sweet."

Walk stared at her. He felt his face turn hot. He wheeled away and stalked up the path.

When he came into the open, the Cheyennes were breaking camp. The tents were down and they were loading them on travois—a pair of poles, one attached to each side of a saddle girth with rawhide; the poles would be dragged behind the horse, which would be ridden probably by a squaw and one or two babies; and behind the horse's heels, the tent and blankets and few belongings would be lashed between the poles.

Ramón was at the back of his wagon, watching northeast. Walk turned. There was a dust cloud a few miles away. He watched it for a moment, and decided it was a herd of horses. Farther behind, moving more slowly, was a small herd of cattle. He turned back and went to his wagon. It looked as if business were coming. Estacado came in riding Agathy and leading the sorrel. Walk got something out of the wagon and dropped it in a saddlebag.

It was near noon when the herds stopped half a mile from the camp. Estacado watched them for a moment and said, "Kiowas. Sometimes they have good stock."

Presently a party of three Indians took off in a lope toward the camp. They wore only breechclouts and moccasins. They came directly to Ramón's wagon. The comancheros gathered around them. Walk and Estacado were on the fringe of the group.

"We have much fine horses—fat cows—to trade," said one Kiowa. He was short and powerfully built, like the Comanches, and bronze like them, with a square face and distinctly hawklike nose, and he sat a magnificent blue roan stallion and looked at them haughtily. His pride held pathos, for Walk was strongly aware that the Kiowa-Comanches had been lords of the Llano Estacado and a great surrounding area for many years by virtue of their superb horsemanship and individual fighting qualities. Now they had been pushed back until the Llano itself was their only free range, and they were reduced to stealing from the ranchmen for outlet of their magnificent energy and abilities, and to haggling with the comancheros for bread to replace buffalo meat, and for colored cloth in place of the buckskin that was no longer plentiful.

It was doubly sad, thought Walk, for there had been so much fuss raised the last few years, in New Mexico Territory and in the Texas Legislature, that the redskins' days even on the Llano indubitably were numbered. He knew, too, that the Indians on the Llano, having nowhere else to go, would fight back hard. There would be violence and death on a big scale. In the end, the Indians would lose, and those left would be confined to reservations little better than prisons.

90

Walk was roused from his momentary reflection by Ramón's sneering answer to the Kiowa: "Flying Bear, your horses are so old they won't carry squaws; your cattle are so thin the buzzards won't pick at them. You keep the good horses for yourself."

"It is always so the comancheros talk."

There was a pause. The circle of men widened around the Indians, and Ramón walked slowly and impudently around the spokesman, examining the horse the Kiowa was riding, while the Indian remained gravely inscrutable. "That blue roan stallion you're on," Ramón said finally, "looks wind-broken, and he's mule-hipped and cow-hocked, but I give you a new bowie knife for him."

"This very fine horse to me," the Kiowa said imperturbably. "He's no good to you—too many things wrong. I keep him."

Walk recognized this as preliminary sparring, but the mention of the blue roan stallion caught his ear. That was the kind of horse the girl had used as an excuse for stopping him down in the Yellowhouse canyon. He moved around and shouldered in a little. There was no brand on the horse's near side. He went around it. On the right hip was a small neat box enclosing a figure three and topped with a rafter—the Three Houses. Walk considered. There was a possibility that the Kiowa had a bill of sale, for it was the usual rule that a horse was never branded more than once, whereas cattle were sometimes burned all over. The bill of sale was a faint possibility, but always present. At any rate, it wasn't his lookout.

Ramón's bowie knife was prominent in the buffalo-calf-tail sheath. There were marks on his face, but he didn't look beaten. And somehow, in the sunlight, he

91

looked taller and not as heavy in the waist as he had last night. He looked leathery and tough and dangerous. He pushed the square black hat back on his head and said, as if not very interested, "We'll go take a look at the rest of your stuff."

The Kiowas wheeled their horses, and Walk watched the blue roan. The other comancheros were scattering to their wagons and their picket horses. Estacado nudged Walk and looked up through his whiskers. "You see how quick Ramón turned away? He's got his eye on the blue roan."

Walk looked at Estacado quizzically. "So have I," he said, and Estacado squirmed.

The comancheros streamed over the prairie. Ramón rode a long-legged coal-black gelding. It was not an especially good horse, Walk thought, for cattle country, but it was certainly a handsome animal, and perhaps excellent for the High Plains, where one might want to travel far and fast.

Walk and Estacado went with the first group. They reached the Kiowas' horse herd, where the animals were held together by half a dozen Indians idly sitting their horses. Walk dismounted and turned the sorrel over to Estacado. He shouldered into the herd. There were a few broomtail mustangs without markings, but most of the animals bore unfamiliar brands. He saw no Tres Casas horses, nor any of the other brands he had seen in the Yellowhouse.

He went back to the three Kiowas. They were already trading with the comancheros indiscriminately, and apparently the horses were in a sort of tribal pool. It was apparent also that the comancheros themselves were observing some sort of order in trading, for Ramón was just concluding a deal with the leader. "Three bowie knives, one bolt of red calico, and twelve sacks of tobacco for my pick of twelve horses," he said.

The Kiowa grunted and nodded. Batty Simpkins stepped up. "Twelve pones of *cemita* bread for six horses," he said.

"No," the Kiowa said gutturally. "Six horses worth twenty loaves."

Walk turned away. Each of the other two Kiowas had a small group of traders around him, all but one in each case awaiting their turn. It began to seem obvious that Walk could not expect his pick of the animals. There did, however, seem to be a limit on each trade. Ramón was the only one who bought more than six horses at a time. At the cattle herd it was the same story. Walk looked at Estacado. Estacado shook his head in discouragement. Walk frowned and went back to the Kiowa leader. Ramón was riding through the herd, selecting horses and cutting them to one side. Diego picked them up and held them in a small group, loose-herded.

Walk waited until it was Ramón's turn again. When the big half-breed started to make another offer, Walk said quietly, "It's my turn, I figger."

Ramón glared at him for a moment. Then he smiled sardonically. "The *tejano* wants to buy," he announced.

Walk stepped up to the Kiowa. "One string of beads," he said, "and one tin bucket for one horse."

Ramón laughed as if in great glee. "The *tejano* buys one horse!" he shouted. "Big businessman—no?"

Walk said quietly, "There's nothing worth buying left in that herd." There was a glint in his eye, but Ramón laughed again.

It seemed to Walk the comancheros were buying pretty cheap, but the Indians were agreeable, and when it came Walk's turn again there were no horses left in the herd. He did buy twelve cattle, for there the limit was double. But Estacado shook his head ominously. "You shore ain't gettin' nothin' but crow bait out of this," he said.

"There will be other days," Walk pointed out. "And I won't always be last. You keep your eye peeled. Before this day is over, the Indians will know me clear up to the Cimarron."

"You gonna a start fireworks?"

Walk was enigmatic. "Not necessarily."

It was his turn for the third time, and there were no animals left in either herd. Ramón, waiting, grinned triumphantly. "You don' do so well, eh? Too bad, *tejano.*"

Walk stiffened. He was often called a Texan, but Ramón's sarcastic drawl and the heavy emphasis he put on the second syllable were calculated to be insulting. But Walk held his temper. He sauntered over to the Kiowa and looked approvingly at the bluc roan. "That's a fine horse," he said. "I like him. I give you one bolt of calico with purple flowers, one sack of tobacco, and one alarm clock for him."

The Kiowa had been about to shake his head, but when he heard "alarm clock" he was interested. He said, "No savvy alarm clock."

Walk turned to his sorrel. He looked at Ramón, saw that he was swelling up, and smiled. He opened a saddlebag and took out a cardboard box. He opened the box before the Kiowa. He pushed the tissue paper to all four sides and revealed a shining nickel-plated creation. He held it up in one hand. The Kiowa reached for it.

"Wait," said Walk. He wound the alarm. He turned the big hand until the thing went off with a fearful clatter that made the roan rear against the bridle. The Kiowa began to grin. He reached for it, but Walk turned it off and said, nodding, "I trade you for the horse—no?"

The Kiowa grunted and nodded eagerly. Walk gave him the clock. He walked over to the blue roan and took off the Indian's saddle. He used his own *mecate* to make a hackamore for the stallion. The Kiowa hurried back to the Indian camp, and the entire tribe gathered around him. Walk listened to the loud, insistent ringing of the bell. He finished the hackamore and turned to Ramón. The big half-breed had moved over to his own group of animals, held by Diego, but at that moment looked at the Kiowa camp and scowled blackly. Walk grinned and called to him, "For a *tejano*, I don' do so bad, eh, boss?"

For a moment he thought the half-breed would explode into violence, but finally Ramón turned away without looking at him. Ramón swung onto his own horse and cut at it viciously with the ends of the reins. The horse jumped forward in a gallop.

Estacado pushed his mule over to where Walk was examining the roan. He looked after Ramón, who was rapidly pulling away. "I'd hate to be in his boots," he muttered. "He's as full of poison as a diamondback rattlesnake. If he bites himself, he'll turn purple and bust." Estacado looked down at Walk. "But I'd hate worse to be in yours," he said.

Walk pretended not to hear him. "That's a right nice piece of horse meat," he said of the blue roan.

"He smells too much like Indian," said Estacado.

Walk looked at Estacado. "Sometimes you don't smell so good yourself." Estacado looked stricken. Walk continued, "If you'd been raised up here on the Plains, with nothing to eat but meat, and you had to gut buffalo and antelope wherever you could find it, and no water to wash in, maybe the Indians would stay upwind of you." He turned back to the horse. "He'll be as fresh and sweet-smelling as an apple blossom in a day or two."

But Estacado had something on his mind. "It's none o' my business," he said, "but d'you figger the brown-haired filly down there in the canyon is worth gittin' Ramón so mad at you for? He planned on gettin' that, blue roan hisself."

Walk straightened. "Ramón was already mad at me," he said. "He was born mad. He's waitin' for an excuse to clean my plow on his terms, so I might as well get something out of it first. Besides, you saw what I got out of those herds today. What kind of a spread can I make out of a bunch of scrubs? I want first pick at some of this stuff—and I'll get it from now on—when the rest of the Indians see that Kiowa's alarm clock." He looked over toward the Kiowa camp. The alarm clock went off again, and Walk chuckled. "That there's known as advertising," he said. Then he looked thoughtfully at Estacado. "She ought to be right pleased to get her bronc back, don't you figger?" he asked softly.

CHAPTER 9

THEY HERDED THEIR HANDFUL OF STOCK AROUND THE comanchero camp to the south of the red hill. There were a number of small herds scattered over the prairie, and they would have to drive out beyond them all for grass. He left Estacado with the animals while he rode back to the wagon and gathered up the items he had agreed to trade the Kiowas. He took a turn out to the

Indian camp, but all the bucks were gone. A buxom young squaw with wide black eyes, who didn't look like a Kiowa, told him they had spotted a small herd of buffalo down the draw a couple of miles and had gone for meat.

He left the items for Flying Bear. He rode back to camp, took the carbine from under the front seat of the wagon, saw that it was loaded, and put it in the saddle scabbard. The wind was in the northwest. He gathered all the gunny sacks he had around the wagon, including the one in which he kept his razor and shaving things, and went to where Estacado was holding their few head of stock. They turned them southwest and went about four miles from camp, where there was plenty of open grass, and hobbled animals with halves of gunny sack folded diagonally.

Walk examined the blue roan thoroughly. "I figger he weighs about twelve hundred," he said. "That's all right for a stallion. He's got a good clear eye and short ears." He backed off a little. "Wide chest, strong shoulders, and plenty of muscle in the quarters. Good hefty barrel." He stepped up and put his hand near the stallion's flank. "Close-coupled, too. What do you think, Estacado?"

"That there's one of the nicest hunks of horse flesh on the Plains," Estacado said promptly. "He's got ev'rything, includin' looks. He's as good a bronc as the California sorrel, and a lot heavier horse. For this country he's got it all over Ramón's black. But what do you care what he's like? You didn't buy him to ride, anyway." Then he said softly: "A buck antelope just walked over the rise to the south. I don't think he's seen us in here with the horses. He's grazin' away from us now."

Walk's eyes fastened on the antelope. It was turned

97

away from them, and only the white patch on its rump showed where it was. Its head bobbed up once, then it went on feeding. Walk drew his carbine from the saddle scabbard. He walked toward the antelope slowly and carefully, keeping one eye on the animal and the other eye on the few steers in their herd. He didn't know how wild the steers were; they might charge if they noticed him on foot.

The antelope's head bobbed up. It was a buck with nice horns—about a seven-year-old, he figured—and it would be good eating if he could get in a killing shot and not have to run it down. At the moment that was impossible, but the animal would turn sidewise presently and present a better target. He froze as the antelope's head came up, with the two single horns standing up straight from its head and curved over at the top toward each other, like prongs. He stood motionless until the antelope began to feed again, then once more he started forward. The antelope lifted its the head again. It was nervous.

Walk motioned to Estacado, who brought the sorrel to him. He gave his tall hat to Estacado, took the sorrel's bridle, and pushed the horse forward so that he was hidden by its neck and front legs. They went ahead slowly. The buck began to feed. It would be all right now unless the wind changed.

When he was within two hundred yards, he let the sorrel's reins trail and he flattened out on the ground. The grass was eighteen inches tall, and hid him effectively. He began to belly forward, dragging the carbine. It was slow, and the sun was hot, but the thought of antelope tenderloin and antelope hams made his mouth water. He kept his head just high enough to watch the white flag. The animal half turned. Walk was

98

within a hundred yards. He brought the rifle up carefully, got it into position. The antelope raised its head, poised for flight. Walk aimed just under the horn and pulled the trigger.

The antelope bounded away with a great leap, but Walk heard the bullet hit, and he did not think the buck would go very far. It didn't. It ran a hundred yards and suddenly piled up in the grass. Walk mounted the sorrel and went forward. The heavy slug had gone through the antelope's head and left a big hole, and the animal was flat on its side, dead. He pulled out a big jackknife. He cut out the seeds, then skinned it. The woolly, pungent-smelling hide he laid to one side. On that he piled the hams, backbone, forequarters, and lights. Three buzzards were wheeling high overhead. He looked to the east and saw a dozen circling one spot; the Kiowas must have taken some buffalo. There was a single buzzard high in the southeast, and he concluded that Pegleg Popham's body had been about cleaned. He wiped the knife blade with grass and dropped the knife in his pocket. He tied the corners of the antelope hide together with a rawhide thong from his vest pocket; then, hoisting the hide, he mounted and rode back, surprising a pair of coyotes skulking in the grass.

Estacado had all the stock hobbled by that time, and they turned to camp. "These gents graze their ridin' stock north of the draw," Estacado said, "so they can ride back and forth." When they were within a mile, Estacado sat up straight on his mule. "Looks like we got company."

Walk studied their wagon at the near end of the street. It was getting along in the afternoon, and he realized they had been gone quite a while. "Looks like the Kiowas," he said. "Half a dozen of 'em. They must of sent the squaws down to skin out the buffalo, but what do you reckon the bucks are doin' at our wagon?"

Estacado said glumly, "You can be mighty sure they didn't come fer tea."

But Walk brightened. "Maybe they're not the same ones at all. Maybe some others have come to trade cows for alarm clocks." He grinned expansively at Estacado. "It pays to advertise. I *told* you."

"There's another bunch up there huntin' for old iron where Popham's wagon was burned," Estacado observed. "I reckon Ramón traded 'em that so they could make arrowheads."

"The wind has swept away the ashes," Walk noted.

Estacado jogged along on his mule, and for a moment there was no sound but that of Walk's gloves slapping against the saddle; then Estacado said reflectively: "In a lot of ways I like to ride a mule. They ain't as fast as a horse, but they last longer. Agathy can singlefoot all day and never get tired."

Walk grunted. He was thinking about the blue roan.

"You take a horse," Estacado went on. "A good horse is more human than some people. But just when you figger you got a mule pegged, he doubles back on the trail and leaves you up in the air."

"You mean," said Walk, finally looking up, "you can't trust a mule like you can a horse."

"I reckon that's it. Leastways, you never get to be friends with a mule because you never know what it's thinking." He looked keenly at Walk from under the brim of his ragged old hat. "Like them Indians up there around our wagon now," he said.

Walk came alive in a hurry. He glanced at Estacado and then at the wagon. He studied the Indians, sitting their horses in a semicircle around the ashes of the campfire. "I reckon you said something, all right," he said in a moment. "Those redskins act as if they're waiting for me to give them something. You reckon that little squaw forgot to turn over that stuff to Flying Bear?"

Estacado shook his head pessimistically. "No Kiowa squaw forgets anything like that," he said positively. "They ain't like these here modern women—"

"Don't talk so loud," Walk said. "You might be talkin' about the lady I'm going to marry."

But he was serious as they approached the Mucha Que campground. The Indians did not act like Indians with stock to sell. Walk and Estacado cut around the foot of the red cliff and were out of sight for a moment. When they came out into the open again, Walk got a shock. The Kiowas had been half lying, with their arms crossed on their horses' necks and their heads resting on their arms. But Agathy shied as they came out from around the cliff near the Indians. She snorted. The Indians straightened up together. One of them was Flying Bear.

The chief's square bronze face and his hawk nose were not reassuring. The thought came over Walk that Flying Bear had decided he wanted the blue roan stallion back. That was bad for two reasons: one was that Walk intended to give the stallion to the girl in the Yellowhouse canyon; the other was that a man couldn't start trading back with the Indians, or there would never be a final deal. And yet, Walk noted, Flying Bear had brought plenty of help; Walk counted five Indians with him.

It was late afternoon. Walk rode through the circle. He alighted at the front of the wagon, threw Dulce's reins over the tongue, and walked around to the back end and dropped the meat on the ground. Estacado rode Agathy around behind the Indians and headed for the draw.

Walk glanced quickly up the row of wagons and carts. Nobody was in sight but Quita, sitting behind Ramón's wagon on a piece of canvas, weaving a horsehair rope. She looked up and caught his eye, then looked down again. He could read nothing in her glance.

He went back to the sorrel, took the rifle from the scabbard, put another cartridge in the magazine, and set it against the front wagon wheel; he settled his revolver in its holster and somewhat ostentatiously cleaned his knife blade again with a handful of grass. Then he swept away the ashes of the morning's fire and got a shovel out of the wagon to dig a pit. He went to the little pile of brush, picked up a small handful and laid it over the pit. He set a couple of dry buffalo chips on top of the brush. Then he took the packet of matches from one pocket of his spotted wildcat vest, raised his right leg, and drew the match across the seat of his pants. It sputtered for a long time, shot out streams of blue smoke, and smelled bitingly of sulphur, but it finally burst into flame. The Indians watched gravely, silently.

Estacado came back with two long chinaberry branches, each forked at one end. He had trimmed off the leaves and sharpened the ends. He tied Agathy to the rear wheel on the side away from the fire, where she would not get wind of the Indians. Walk went to the back end of the wagon. He lifted a peg and pulled out the long steel wagon rod that held up the tail gate. It was sharp on one end. He went over to the fire and used the wagon rod to make holes in the ground, rounding the holes out at the top with a circular motion of the rod.

Estacado came and worked the sharp ends of the branches into the holes until they were solid. Walk knocked the dirt off the wagon rod and worked the sharp end through the meat on one of the antelope hams. When he had the ham spitted on the rod, he set the rod on the forked sticks just over the fire. Estacado got out the frying pan and began to stir up some dough. Walk tied up the rest of the antelope meat and hung it from the tailboard. Finally he rubbed his hands in the red dirt to clean them. He dusted them off on the seat of his pants. Then he turned to Flying Bear. "You had good luck with the buffalo—yes?"

Flying Bear nodded. "We kill two," he said. "Is good meat—not like antelope."

Walk nodded. It made him feel better to know they probably would not hang around to help eat the antelope. He said no more. The twigs burned down, and the buffalo chips began to burn with a blue, almost invisible flame. Walk sat on his spurs before the fire and stared into it, pretending to be lost in absorption. Estacado worked the frying pan into the fire and went down to the draw for water.

The Indians were looking at each other. Finally Flying Bear spoke.

At first Walk was relieved to know he had won the opening round, but an instant later, realizing what the Kiowa was saying, he froze.

"We want whisky," Flying Bear said in an uncompromising tone.

For a moment Walk was speechless. So it was true the comancheros at this camp were in the habit of trading whisky to the Indians! He remembered the accusation by the girl in the Yellowhouse. He also realized he was probably the only comanchero at Mucha

Que who had no whisky to offer. He thought fast. His answer would have to be good.

He looked up. "I did not promise whisky," he said. "I promised cloth, beads, tobacco, an alarm clock. At those I have given according to my word."

Flying Bear considered for a moment. "At Mucha Que," he said, "is always whisky with every deal. You tell us now where to find whisky, we go."

Walk gazed at him. He could see now why the comancheros had bought so cheaply that morning. He remembered again Quita's words. It was understood that with every deal went so much whisky, which would be delivered after the Indians were too far away from Mucha Que to raid the traders herds and take back the stock.

Walk shook his head. "I have no whisky," he said firmly, but he knew with certainty that Flying Bear would not go away empty-handed. He arose to his full length. "I am new here," he said. "I did not know about this, and I have no whisky—but I will give you something else." He went to the wagon and got something out of a box. He went up to Flying Bear and handed him another alarm clock of shining brass and gleaming nickel plate. "Will this make us square?" he asked.

Flying Bear took the clock. His face did not change, but his eyes lost some of their gravity. Walk thought he was disappointed but a little pleased. There was rapid talk between Flying Bear and the Indian on his right, in Kiowa, and at the end of the interchange Flying Bear handed the clock to the other Kiowa, whose face expanded with delight. He immediately manipulated it until it broke out in a shrill ring, and then laughed as the other bucks crowded around him. Walk sat down on his spurs again.

But Flying Bear did not offer to leave. There was talk among them, and the chief's pony moved a step closer to Walk. "I make a deal," he said. "I trade you a nice slave girl." He held up his right hand, with the bronze fingers wide-spread. "Five gallons whisky," he said, "for a nice slave girl like Quito." Walk stared up at him, too astonished to answer immediately. The Kiowa grinned ingratiatingly. "How you like that little squaw at camp—yes?"

Walk got to his feet slowly. So this was it. He knew the Indians had done a good deal of slave trading before the war, but he hadn't realized it was still carried on. Also, he saw that Flying Bear thought Walk was merely driving a hard bargain. That was doubly bad.

He looked squarely at Flying Bear and said plainly: "I cannot do that, for I have no whisky. You don't need it anyway, for you will have plenty from the other comancheros. And I cannot buy a slave. Slavery is against the law."

There was silence for a moment. The six Kiowas looked steadily at him. He saw hostility growing in their bronze faces. He held himself tightly. One young Indian grunted: "The others give whisky. This one cheats. He's *tejano—no bueno!*"

Flying Bear delivered his verdict with narrowed eyes. He said gutturally: "You no trade like the others. You no want slaves. You talk of law. What you here for anyhow?"

"I'm here to do an honest business," said Walk, "to trade for stock."

"You no comanchero," said Flying Bear, "You come here to spy for the Army—no?"

"If I did," Walk pointed out, "I'd keep my mouth

105

shut."

He watched the Indians swell up with indignation and growing hatred, and he waited, his gun hand ready. Flying Bear snorted his disgust, then wheeled his pony and rode off. They all followed, slouched in their seats, legs and arms dangling.

Estacado spoke in a low voice at Walk's elbow. "You reckon we can find anybody else around here to get cross-ways with?"

Walk looked at him. He smiled ruefully and said, "We can try."

CHAPTER 10

WITH TIGHT LIPS WALK WATCHED THE SMALL FIRE. Although it wasn't necessary yet, he reached out and took hold of the eyed end of the wagon rod and turned the meat. Estacado sat cross-legged, watching the Indians disappear in the draw.

"Slavery!" Walk said finally. "We just fought a war over slavery. If the Federals catch you holding anybody in slavery, they can fine you thousands of dollars and throw you in a penitentiary for nobody knows how many years." He took a deep breath. "But it looks like the Indians and the comancheros are dealing in slaves right and left. No wonder they don't like pilgrims out here."

Estacado said, "If you was as righteous about brands as you are about murder and slavery, we wouldn't be in this mess."

Walk stared at the fire and said nothing.

"But," Estacado went on, "we can't pull out of here now. They'd figger sure you were running away, and the next thing you and me would know, St. Peter would be shovin' a grubbin' hoe in our hands and tellin' us to go cut some firewood."

Walk swallowed. He was suddenly aware that his throat hurt from tenseness. "We've got only one chance," he said. "We've got to stay right here and keep trading to quiet their suspicions."

"That there's the smartest thing you said today."

"Slavery," Walk muttered. "Do you suppose—" He got up and looked toward Ramón's wagon.

Estacado's weatherbeaten face turned pale beneath his whiskers. He croaked, "If you go mixin' in Ramón's business, you'll never get a taste of this ham."

Walk was looking over the street. "Ramón and Diego went over toward the Kiowa village a little while ago," he said. "The other traders are out checkin' up on their stock for the night." His gray eyes were searching the encampment of Mucha Que. "I'm just going to ask her. They said 'a slave girl like Quita,' but they might be bluffing, too. She might be Ramón's squaw."

Estacado looked at him steadily. "You got any folks back home?" he asked.

Walk grinned at him. "Sing 'Rock of Ages' for me, and turn this outfit over to the first needy mule skinner you see."

But Estacado didn't smile.

Walk strode up the street between the wagons, his spurs jingling. Quita was at the back end of Ramón's wagon, working on the horsehair rope. She looked up questioningly and then continued with her task, her bronze fingers moving swiftly and efficiently as she interwove the strands. A kettle of soup was simmering over a fire. Walk leaned against the big rear wheel and said casually, "What tribe you belong to, Quita?"

The brown hands grew still. She looked toward the west, then up at Walk, and her brown eyes were misty.

"I was Pah-Ute two-three years ago," she said.

"How did you get so far from home?"

"Apaches raid my village; take me and my sister. They keep me many months, move me many places, take my sister away, then take me to Las Lenguas and sell me to the beeg boss."

Walk's eyes widened. "Then you are not Ramón's squaw?"

Her eyes flashed. She jerked at the horsehair. "No— and is good. Ramón beats me, but he is careful not to leave bad marks, because the beeg boss would keel him!"

"Why doesn't the big boss keep you with him?"

She frowned. "I don' know. He buys me a month ago from the Apaches, but he sends me here with Ramón and tells Ramón to take care of me, he weel come for me after the Comanche moon."

He tried to trick her by asking in Spanish, *"Quién es el caporal grande?"* (Who is the big boss?)

But she shrugged and answered as she had the day before, *"Yo no sé."*

"What does he look like?"

She glanced up. "Beeg," she said. "Tall as you, but wide. He wears red calf vest, and has brown hair smooth like scales on snake."

Walk took a deep breath. "I met a big bruiser like that," he said, "and he was a fit brother for a sidewinder." He looked at her. "Do you like him?" he asked.

She shuddered. "He's more worse than Ramón," she said.

Walk went back to Estacado and told him what he

had learned. "It sure sounds like slavery to me."

"Why don't this fellow take the Indian girl, then? Why does he leave her here?"

"I got it figured this way," said Walk. "Supposin' the big boss *is* this bruiser down in the Yellowhouse. He's got his eye on that little filly down there, for besides bein' a right handsome lady, it seems to be her father that owns the Tres Casas brand which runs in the upper end of the canyon. The big bruiser sees this Indian girl, and he wants her. He figgers he can buy her cheap and no questions asked; later on he can take her to his ranch and put her to work as a cook or something, but in the meanwhile he don't dare, because the filly in the Yellowhouse would heave him clean out of the corral if he showed up with an Indian girl."

"That seems to spell out that he's tryin' to get the lady in the Yellowhouse to marry him."

"That's what it spells," said Walk.

Estacado looked at him. "Maybe the blue roan wasn't any use to you after all."

Walk pointed out, "He mighta ast her, but she hadn't said yes or he wouldn't of let her come to meet us by herself."

Estacado snorted. "His kind," he said, "is liable to do anything. They got the brain action of a Gila monster." Then he delivered an opinion: "One thing is sure: Ramón is just the *segundo*. No matter how you take care of Ramón, you'll have to answer to the big boss. You take my advice and don't even ask any more questions."

"I think I know where everybody stands now," said Walk, "and I don't need to ask any more questions." He went on thoughtfully: "I don't doubt there's plenty of honest traders among the comancheros—or they would be honest if they could be—but it's this gent behind

109

Ramón who is responsible for the lawlessness. No doubt he puts up the money for a lot of these fellows to operate. Then he pays them a dollar or two a head for what they turn over, and he shoves the stuff on out to New Mexico or up to Colorado Territory and sells it to people who aren't too fussy. He's the dangerous man in this business, for he's got a lot at stake and he's violating just about every law on the books, one way or another."

"I wish I was back in the Pecos country," Estacado moaned. "This here is like carryin' a keg of black powder with a lighted fuse through a rattlesnake den to fight a couple of hungry grizzlies."

"Don't worry about me talkin' to her," Walk said with assurance. "The camp is practically deserted."

"If that is so," said Estacado, and jerked his head past Walk's shoulder, "you got any idea why Ramón and Diego happen to be ridin' up from the draw this minute?"

Walk turned around. There was purpose in Ramón's riding. He sat forward in the saddle but held the big black horse back with a harsh rein that twisted the horse's neck to the rear and kept its mouth open as it gasped against the pain of the Spanish bit.

Walk moved to the other side of the fire where he could watch all approaches except from the west, which was covered by the red cliff at his back. He glanced up casually as Ramón made for his own wagon. A slight frown came between his eyes as Ramón disappeared past the line of wagons. He sat back on his heels and took out his big .44 Army Colt, He broke it, looked at the percussion caps of all the cartridges, clicked it back together, and spun the cylinder. Then he chucked it back into his holster and reached out to turn the meat.

Estacado watched all this, and his face looked pinched.

Walk's eyes ostensibly were on the fire, but he was listening to every sound on the prairie and seeing every movement within his line of vision. His senses had become abnormally keen; he saw buzzards settling over the draw a couple of miles east, and knew the squaws had finished cleaning the buffalo. The Indians would eat long and heartily that night. He heard a sound like the distant buzzing of a rattlesnake, and knew it came from a brood of young burrowing owls underground somewhere nearby; he felt a distant thudding on the ground, and knew a jack was whipping a stallion into submission; he smelled burning willow bark, and knew an Indian down in the draw had lit a cigarette. He took in all those small impressions and a dozen others, almost without knowing it, and interpreted them without a conscious effort to do so, while he waited for sight or sound of Ramón coming to face him.

He should have known that Ramón was too shrewd to attack directly without the moral support of his followers. He heard the thump of Ramón's boots on the hard ground, and heard words in high-pitched Spanish. The volume of Ramón's voice was held low, and Walk could not distinguish the words, but even in the smooth Spanish tongue Ramón managed to impart an explosive quality that foreshadowed violence.

Walk was surprised when it came. He heard a loud smack, and Ramón shouted in a voice almost out of control, *"Hija de siete millones—"* as Quita, suddenly propelled across the ground back of the wagon, stumbled backward, vainly trying to recover her balance and to keep from falling. She tripped over a tarpaulin and went down. Ramón was after her. He seized her arm and jerked her to her feet. "Run from me, eh? Run from

111

Ramón?" He spun her around by the arm and launched his body against her as she turned. She fell in a heap.

Knots formed at the corners of Walk's jaws. Estacado watched him apprehensively. "Remember what she said," he told Walk. "He won't hurt her bad. He don't dare."

Walk didn't answer. The girl was getting up. Ramón slapped her with his right hand open, then with his left. The blows would not, perhaps, leave deep marks, but they were brutal. They sounded loud in Walk's ears, and he opened his mouth and sucked in a deep breath. Ramón had her arm again. His eyes glittered. He swung harder and threw her crashing into the wagon. Walk got to his feet. He heard her sobbing. He stood for a moment, working his lower jaw.

But a sudden and unexpected turn came in the fight. Ramón had darted in after her, but now he backed away with his arms before his face. "No!" His voice was a sound of abject terror. They saw why. Quita was running at him with a tin plate full of burning coals that she had scooped from the fire. He stared at her as if hypnotized until she threw them into his face; then he uttered a hoarse, inarticulate cry and fled through the mesquite toward the draw.

Walk smiled and sat down. "It seems Ramón doesn't care for fire," he observed.

Estacado was watching the spot of Ramón's disappearance with open mouth. "I ain't never seen the like of that," he said finally. "He's skeered to death of it. He's absolutely scared ess-spitless." He shook his bushy head incredulously. "I've seen horses go crazy when a corral caught fire, but I never seen a man do it before."

Walk was sober again. "That's only one time," he said. "She won't always have a fire handy. And besides,

112

there's no guarantee he won't give her a whipping for throwing the coals at him. He's got a streak of cruelty as wide as the Brazos River."

They had not long to wait. Diego followed his master to the draw, leading the black, and presently again they came up out of the mesquite. Ramón was slashing the black with a quirt. Walk felt the knots rising in his jaws again. "He's decided to risk it," he said tensely. "He'll beat her up and then tell her owner she tried to run away."

Ramón disappeared behind the wagon. A moment later came the crack of a rawhide whip on buckskin and open flesh. The girl gave a little scream, and then she was silent while the whip continued to fall. There was a pounding of horse's hoofs, and Ramón screamed, "Hold her, Diego!"

Walk cringed with the next blow. Then Ramón's voice, choked with sadistic fury, shouted, "Take off her dress!"

Walk rolled to his feet. He strode forward. Estacado was at his side, holding the rifle cradled in his arms. They went down the street. Walk felt as if he were walking on something round and rubbery, but his gun arm hung loose at his side.

They were in the center of the street. Batty Simpkins was watching, glaze-eyed, while Diego tore at the girl's leather jacket. Diego was old, and the girl was struggling hard, making it a difficult job for him.

Estacado fell in behind Walk with the rifle, and Walk said through thin lips, "Ramón, I come to trade with you." Diego heard the flat deadliness in his voice, and stopped. The girl pulled her half-torn buckskin waist around her welted shoulders and turned away, sobbing quietly, and stood waiting.

113

Ramón swelled up. Then he got control of himself; the glitter left his eyes and was replaced by a calculating gleam. "You want a squaw, eh, *tejano?*"

Walk held his temper. "I'll take her off your hands," he said quietly.

Ramón was derisive. "You the one who said slavery against the law."

"I'll make you a trade," Walk repeated stonily.

Ramón's eyes turned crafty. "What you got to trade for a squaw like this?" His hands described curves. "So *simpática!*" he said lustfully.

Walk was unmoved. He said, "I'll trade you a horse."

Ramón's black eyes lighted up. "The sorrel—yes?"

Walk said harshly, "I wouldn't trade you the sorrel to whip the way you're whipping this girl, but I'll trade you a horse that's every bit as much horse as the sorrel—and able to fight back." He paused to get his breath. "I'll trade you the blue roan," he said.

Ramón froze into immobility for a moment. He looked at Walk to see if Walk meant it. Then he licked his grayish lips.

Walk met his stare. Ramón's eyes shifted. He looked off toward the southwest, then back at Walk.

"Maybe I trade," he said, "but I whip the squaw first. I have tell her not to talk to strangers."

Walk said, "No. You trade first."

Ramón looked at Walk, trying to estimate his determination. "What do you say if I whip her first, *tejano?*"

Walk said, without any show of emotion, "I'll fill you full of bullet holes up one side and down the other and lace you up with a strip of rawhide." He smiled coldly. "You been calling me *tejano*. You want to find out?"

Ramón's cheeks became heavy. His big shoulders

moved as he breathed. Finally he said in a harsh whisper, "O.K. We trade."

Walk jerked his head at the southwest. "You know where he is. Send your man to cut him out." He spoke to Quita. "Get your things."

She was looking up at him, her eyes large and soft and wondrous. She nodded briefly, quickly. "*Sí, señor.*" She snatched a blanket from the tailboard of the wagon. "We go now?" she asked.

Walk nodded without looking at her. He gave Ramón one final sweeping stare and turned away. When he got to the end of the street, he looked back. Estacado was leaning against the front wheel of Ramón's wagon, the rifle still across his arms. Ramón growled an order in Spanish at Diego. The straw-hatted Mexican jumped into his saddle and began fogging southwest. Estacado caught Walk's eye, got up and sauntered back.

Quita put her blanket on the tailboard of Walk's wagon, as if that were undeniably where it was supposed to be, and made herself busy on the other side of the wagon, partially out of sight. Perhaps, Walk thought, she was sewing some buttons—or whatever she used for buttons—back on her buckskin bodice.

Estacado put the rifle under the seat. He looked at Walk and rolled his eyes toward the back end of the wagon. "Now you got her," he said, "what air you goin' to do with her?"

Walk went over to the fire and turned the ham. "How in thunderation do I know?"

"I never took you fer no squaw man."

"I'm not." He looked into the small fire and frowned.

"You haven't done nothing to put yourself in good with the brown-haired filly down in the Yellowhouse, either—tradin' her pet horse for an Indian girl."

115

Walk said, without looking up: "I thought of that. There's just some things I can't stand." He frowned again. "Ramón found out what I said about slavery in a hurry, didn't he?"

"You got these fellers scared. I reckon a good many of 'em are more or less guilty. But that ain't the least of your trouble. What are you goin' to do with her?"

"That's one question I can answer," Walk said, and now there was assurance in his voice. "I'll give her her freedom and let her go back to the Paiutes."

There was silence for a moment. The cooking meat smelled good. Then a drop of juice sizzled in the fire.

Estacado observed: "You got a big turnover, son, but I don't exactly figure where your profit's comin' from. You swapped one bolt of calico with purple flowers and one sack of tobacco and two alarms clocks fer a hoss the like of which you won't see again in a month of Sundays. You swapped the horse for Quita back there. You're sendin' Quita home. How long do you figger your alarm clocks arc goin' to hold out at that rate?"

Walk sighed.

Estacado went on remorselessly, "And that still ain't your biggest problem. That's comin' when the big boss finds out you took her away from him."

"That will be Ramón's problem."

"Don't be any funnier'n you've been already. Ramón will swear you made him trade at the point of a six-shooter, and then the six-shooter'll be pointed at you." Estacado moistened his lips. "I figger your life expectancy is gettin' mighty short, son—mighty short."

Walk got up and reached for a mesquite root to lay in the coals. But as his arm stretched down, a soft brown hand touched his, and Quita's gentle voice said: "*No, señor*, this is woman's work. Quita will do this."

116

He took a deep breath and turned to look at her. He watched her carefully push the mesquite burl into the center of the coals from the side. He watched her turn the antelope ham over and scrutinize it quickly to see if the outside was cooked all the way around to seal in the juices. Then she turned it to a spot that suited her. She got the big leather bucket and went down to the draw. Walk watched her go. Her step was light, and gave no hint that she had just been beaten. Walk said, "She's got a lot of bounce."

Estacado said thoughtfully: "I just remembered something. She didn't belong to Ramón anyway, so she doesn't belong to you now. So you can't free her."

"You've forgotten something too. She can't legally belong to anybody. I just gave Ramón a horse to turn her loose, that's all. When she gets back, I'll tell her she's free."

"I got a hunch," Estacado said slowly, "this isn't going to turn out the way you might want it to." He got up. "The sun is beginnin' to get low. I'm hungry."

"Me too," said Walk.

"I'll stoke up a little frying-pan bread," said Estacado.

But he had hardly started when two slim brown hands pushed his aside. Quita said: "I will make the meals. You go sit down, like big chief."

"I ain't no Injun," Estacado spluttered.

"You have fine whiskers," she said imperturbably. "I call you Chief. You go now, and rest."

Walk bit his lip. He watched Estacado from the corner of his eye. The old mountain man was fuming, but he was pleased too.

Walk sat back against the wagon wheel and relaxed. "Better enjoy this while you can," he advised Estacado.

The older man looked at him fiercely through his

whiskers. "I am," he said, "but I shore ain't used to it."

Walk watched the girl make bread. Her hands moved fast and efficiently; she knew what she was doing, and wasted no motions. In a remarkably few minutes she had the pan sitting on the coals. Then she stood before Walk and looked down at him with her soft brown eyes like a doe's. "Is no meat cooked yet," she said. "You want I should get prairie dogs for supper?"

He was amused. "Sure," he said. "Go catch a couple."

The sun was out of sight from the wagon. The rest of the prairie appeared to be still in broad daylight, but the red cliff threw a shadow over their wagon and halfway down the street.

She disappeared behind the red cliff. Estacado chuckled. "She plumb fergot the bread."

Walk said: "I'll watch it. Anyway, it'll be all right for fifteen minutes or so." He looked at Estacado. "I reckon you and I'll have to move our bedroom to the foot of the cliff, there, for tonight."

He was just reaching for the frying-pan handle when a soft voice said, "*No, señor,* that is not work for you."

He looked up. His eyes popped open. Quita was carrying three fat brown prairie dogs by their hind legs.

"How'd you get 'em?" he asked in amazement. "I didn't hear any shots."

"No." She looped a buckskin thong over a dog's hind legs and tied the carcass to a stake at the side of the wagon. "I have set traps every day," she said. "Two of them were caught. The other one I got with this." Her brown hand went to her waist, and a knife materialized in it.

Estacado gasped. "That ain't no lady's knife," he said, moving back a little.

"Is a very good knife," she said.

"That's a full-grown bowie knife," Walk said wonderingly. "But how did you get a prairie dog with it?"

Estacado recovered some of his poise. "You didn't have no salt," he snickered.

Deftly she slit the dog down the belly and began to skin it. "Is a good throwing knife," she said.

Estacado gulped audibly. His head came forward on his short neck. "You mean to say you can stick a dog with that knife—and they duck bullets right along?"

"I do not know about bullets, she said, "but I know about the knife. Is very fast—a knife," she said, matter-of-factly. "Faster than a pistol."

"Why didn't you use that knife on Ramón?"

"I am not so strong as Ramón," she said. "I would hurt him, but he would kill me." She drew the skin over the dog's head. "Tomorrow," she announced, expertly scooping out the lights, "we make prairie-dog soup. You have flour—no? Makes good soup. Today we have meat. You stuff. Tomorrow we have soup. You stuff, eh?" She sliced off the dog's head and tossed it on a tin plate, where it was followed by the two front quarters. She cocked her head and looked at Walk. "You want I should eat prairie dog too?"

"Well, sure," he said. "But look—" He paused painfully, and then blurted, "Tomorrow you won't be here!"

She did not look up at him, and he saw no indication that she was moved by his announcement. "Yes?" she said.

Walk sat back against the wagon wheel. "Tonight," he said decisively, "you will put the other ham on the fire and see that it is cooked, for tomorrow you are going on a long trip, and I don't want you to be hungry."

Her strong brown hands, busy with a prairie dog hanging from the wagon stake, froze for an instant. He saw her red lips part, then close again. She looked at him and said, "We are going on long trip—yes?"

"*You* are," he corrected her.

"*No me quiere?*" she asked quietly.

"Yes, I like you!" he retorted. "Why do you think I traded that blue roan for you?"

"Because you think maybe I am—*simpática.*"

Walk frowned and looked at Estacado. Estacado, studying the fire with abrupt intensity, was wearing a wide smile wholly visible even through his whiskers. Walk looked back at Quita. "Tomorrow you are going back to your people in Utah," he said.

She turned her large brown eyes on him. "But I am your slave—no?"

"You are my slave—no!" he thundered. "Now let's stick to the real facts. First, you are free; second, I don't need a slave."

"*Primeramente,*" she repeated, "I am not free, because you have bought me with a horse—a very fine horse. *Segundamente,* you need a slave to cook and wash for you." She continued cleaning the dog. "You not even know how to catch prairie-dog," she said with unanswerable logic.

But Walk was firm. "You are going home," he repeated.

"*No le gusta yo.*" "I am not pleasing to you," she said with a pleasant little pout.

Walk tried to be calm. "Haven't you got a family back in Utah—mother, father?"

She looked at him again. Her eyes were misty. "*No, señor.* None of my family is left. The Apaches scalped them all." She was thoughtful. "Tell me why you no need slave. You busy trading for cows and horses all day. You no have time to cook supper even."

"I won't always be a comanchero. I'm going to find a place for a ranch—a few sections of grass, a little water."

She studied him. "You look for Lost Spring?" she suggested.

He nodded.

"You have a *señora?*"

"No, but—"

"You theenk you have one all peecked out."

He nodded with a small sigh, thinking this would end it.

"You will need me more than ever," she told him. "The *señora* will have many *niñas*. I help you both." She went on quickly and earnestly: "I your slave. I like to be your slave. *Me gusta mucho.* I not want to go home. You weel let me stay—no?"

"No," Walk said defiantly. "You are not staying. Tomorrow you light out for home. You can ride, can't you?"

"*Sí, señor.*"

"Then tomorrow morning you load up a bunch of meat and take that old crow bait I bought today and light out. *Andale! Sabe?*"

She laid the pieces of the second dog in the frying pan. It was hot and the new pieces sizzled. She moved them around with the point of the bowie knife to make room.

"You send me to die," she informed him sadly. "Can you theenk how far I get alone through Comanche and Kiowa and Apache country? Do you theenk Ramón will let me go? Ramón will never forget that you stopped

121

him from whipping me. He would pay the Apaches well to capture me and keep me until he comes to feenish the beating." She sighed. "It weel not be pleasant, *señor*."

She looked up at him. There were tears in her eyes. "Oh, hell!" said Walk.

CHAPTER 11

THE NEXT MORNING WALK OPENED ONE EYE AND SAW Quita tending the fire. "That antelope smells good," he said. "You reckon she stayed up all night to watch it?"

"She's *your* slave." Estacado pulled on a battered boot. "She don't look like she's plannin' on pullin' out today, either. You'da been better off with the blue roan—if the blue roan could cook."

They went down to the draw. Walk got on his hands and knees and buried his face in the cold water. He took a long drink and came up dripping. "Water tastes good. Not gyppy the way it gets below the Plains."

"What's the matter with the water below the Plains? You can see through it, can't you? You ought to try the Pecos."

Walk regarded him whimsically. "I've seen the Pecos," he said. "I've even drunk from it, and I'm still alive to talk about it—but I'd sure like to find a creek like this that a man could settle on." He watched Estacado drinking, and then asked seriously, "What am I going to do with her?"

Estacado got up; his face also was dripping. "You're beginnin' to repeat yourself something terrible." He squeezed the water out of his whiskers and said, "Put 'er to work."

They picked up the sorrel and the saddle mule from

across the draw and went back to the wagon. The fire was low, and Quita was busying herself with the antelope tenderloin. Estacado picked up a handful of buffalo chips to put on the fire, but almost as he straightened up two small brown hands were on his chest, pushing him back gently but firmly. "You sit down, Chief. I take care of fire."

Walk smiled. "Do what she says—Chief."

Estacado glared at him but sat down, fuming.

The sun came up, a great yellow tub on the horizon. It would be hot again.

"There will be Comanches today, with much horses and cows," Quita announced.

Walk nodded. She knocked out the steaming hot pan bread in a tin plate. Walk sniffed and said, "Smells better'n *your* bread, Chief."

Estacado snorted.

With her bowie knife Quita sliced the pie-shaped bread into two layers. She cut hot, thick slices of antelope meat and covered the bottom layer. She put the top layer on and cut the sandwich in half and offered it to them. Walk shook his head. "Cut some for yourself," he said.

But she refused. "I make more later, when I make dumplings for the soup," she said.

Walk looked around and caught Estacado licking his lips. It annoyed him for a moment. "There's a kettle for you to make soup in, inside the wagon," he told her. "But you better wash out some clothes for us first— what we can spare."

"*Sí, señor,*" she said eagerly. "I wash everything."

They finished breakfast. Estacado licked his fingers. They saddled the animals and headed southwest to look over the stock. Estacado patted his stomach. "Maybe it was a good trade at that."

Their small piece of stock was the farthest from camp of any herd in that vicinity, and Walk spotted a huge gray lobo wolf lying in the grass south of their herd. "He's probably hungry," Walk noted. "Rabbits have been scarce this summer. I reckon he's figuring on a meal off of the herd tonight."

"Gimme the rifle," Estacado said. "My step-pappy was a wolf-hunter. I can fool this critter."

He was shielded by the horses so the wolf could not see him take the rifle. He used a couple of saddle thongs to rig the rifle under the *rosadero,* and rode off on Agathy, apparently in the direction of Mucha Que.

Walk examined the stock, noting also that the wolf did not move or show itself. The blue roan stallion was not with his herd, of course. Walk sighed, but, he reflected, it was in a good cause. All he had to do now was find a way to get Quita back to her own tribe.

He found saddle marks on the broomtail he had traded for. It was a typical scrub mustang, and with no brand marks the Indians themselves might have run it down in the Palo Duro Canyon. He used his *mecate* to fashion a hackamore, and presently got easily on the horse's back and prodded it around a few times. It crowhopped a little on stiff forelegs, but didn't unseat him even barebacked. It guided well with the knees, and he thought probably it had been taken from some other Indian tribe.

Presently he heard a shot, and Estacado rose up out of the grama grass like a whiskered stump. "I got him," he yelled. He went back for Agathy, and came riding up with a broad grin. "It ain't ev'rybody can stalk a lobo on the Plains in broad daylight."

"That was a good piece of work—but why do you

suppose that lobo was up here in the daytime? They generally roam the Plains at night and head for the breaks in the daytime."

Estacado said, "I fergot to ast."

He gave the rifle back to Walk. "These here ain't such a bad bunch of critters," he observed. "They're all Texas cattle, at least, and not Mexican."

Walk agreed. "They're all dark and line-backed and pretty well round-barreled—not as rangy as Mexican cattle. They show a little eastern blood. They must have come from along the foot of the Caprock, but I don't know any of the brands."

"They coulda come from anywhere."

"The three cows might drop some fair calves if I breed them up," Walk said. "That's one of the reasons I brought that twenty-five hundred in the cowhide; when we get all our herd together I'll go up into Colorado and buy a good Durham bull. They cross all right with Longhorns; the calves are hardy and yet they're beefier, too, like a Durham. This bunch of stuff wouldn't win any prizes," he admitted, "but it's only a start. I couldn't lay back and not buy anything."

"It didn't cost you much," said Estacado. "And it isn't worth any more'n it cost."

"I figger those alarm clocks will bring me a better pick of stuff later on. The Indians will put their price higher so the others won't buy so quick. They'll save some of their stuff for me."

"You fergot about the whisky."

"There was a treaty back in the 1840's," said Walk, "and the government agreed that white traders would not bring it in to trade with the Comanches or Kiowas,"

"I reckon the rest of the comancheros never heard of that treaty," Estacado observed, "and maybe the Indians

125

haven't either. They sure wanted whisky yesterday."

"They wanted alarm clocks too. There haven't been hardly any of those things in this part of the country since 1861, when the war began, so I figgered they were good for a novelty."

Estacado got back on his mule. "That's fine. You got a bead on the Indians. Now what are you goin' to do about the comancheros? They ain't going to like it when you start cuttin' into their business."

"There's no rule says you can't offer an Indian an alarm clock for a horse," Walk pointed out.

"Likewise," said Estacado, "there isn't no rule out here to keep a comanchero from sinkin' a knife in your back if he cuts your sign."

"Let's get to camp," said Walk.

When they reached the wagon, Quita was not in sight, but the big kettle was on the fire alongside the second antelope ham, and was about half full of warm water.

"Where's your slave gone—back home to see her folks?"

Walk looked at him. "You take the grubbing hoe and go chop up some mesquite roots," he said. "I'm goin' to use some of that water to shave my face."

"That there," said Estacado, "is knowed as the civilizin' influence of wimmen."

Walk was already looking in the wagon. He had left his razor and shaving things under the seat when he took the gunny sacks, but those implements were not there now. He went to the back of the wagon and looked in under the tarp. The wagon was pretty well loaded, and it was dark under the canvas; he couldn't take the tarp off without untying it, so he crawled halfway in on his stomach, but found nothing. He began to wonder what he had been thinking about when he emptied the things

126

out of the sack. He went to the front of the wagon and crawled under the tarp there. He remembered he would have to trade the Indians out of some rawhide to make hobbles when he got more stock. He didn't want Estacado herding the stuff out there alone, the way they stood with the comancheros. And then there was Quita. If Estacado spent the nights with the herd, Walk would be left alone with the girl. No, he decided he'd use hobbles; they were safer Anyway, he had a bell somewhere; they could use a bell mare, and that would help.

It was stiffing hot under the canvas, and he was about ready to give up when his foot hit a can. Something inside rattled. He picked up the can and took it out with him. Arbuckle's Coffee. He took off the lid. His shaving things were inside. Quita had put them away for him.

He got down from the wagon. He dipped his shaving brush in the warm water and rubbed it over a round cake of soap in his left hand. His small piece of broken mirror was in the can too. He propped it up on the tailboard, took out the coiled-up razor strop, and hit it a few licks with the straightedge: Then he went to work. He finished shaving and rinsed his face with deliciously warm water. Then he heard steps behind him. He turned. Quita was carrying the big leather bucket full of water. It was too big and too heavy for her, and she had to hold it high before her with both hands. She put it down for a moment to rest. He grabbed it up and carried it to the fire.

"You want it in here?"

"Yes—please."

He poured the water in the big kettle. "How much more do you need?"

"One more." She was cutting up a thick cake of lye

127

soap with her bowie knife. He watched the deep yellow chips curl into the warm water. "Why didn't you take the kettle down to the draw to wash?" he asked. "That's not as heavy as all this water."

Her black hair was in braids down both sides of her face, and she brushed a strand away from her forehead with the back of the hand that held the bowie knife. "I do not want to be away so long. You might need me."

Walk said impatiently, "I'll bring the water myself, then."

"I go with you," she said quickly.

"No." His voice was unnecessarily loud. "Stay here and do the washing. I'll bring the water."

"*Sí, señor,*" she said meekly.

He picked up the bucket and strode away. He was trying hard to be displeased, but it wasn't as easy as it should have been.

He followed a. diagonal course northeast that led past Ramón's wagon but at some distance from it. The grass had been grazed off short, and the ground around the camp was pretty dusty. It was not easy walking in the stilted cowboy boots, and every time he set a slanted heel down, the following impact of his boot sole sent out a little puff of dust in all directions.

By the time he reached the crest of the rise, he could hear Estacado swinging the grubbing hoe in the mesquite bushes. He looked around at the camp. The comancheros were busy at their chores: some were mending clothes and harness; others were cooking; one was washing. Ramón seemed to be checking over his trading stock inside his wagon; Batty Simpkins was sitting on his wagon tongue, smoking; Bear Hug Hobart, wearing his coonskin, cap, apparently had just borrowed a grubbing hoe from Ramón and was walking toward

128

the draw; Diego was not to be seen.

Quita was just visible past the tailboard of Walk's own wagon, stirring the clothes with a stick; he could smell the warm, soapy, water. He turned back. To the east there were still a few buzzards over the buffalo carcasses, and far across the Plains a lone rider was smoking a dust trail toward the Kiowa camp. The Kiowas themselves appeared to be leisurely packing up to move.

Walk went down into the draw, through the mesquite bushes, to the small stream. He got down on his stomach for a drink, then he turned the big leather bucket on its side to fill it. He pulled it up dripping, and heard the pounding hoofs of a hard-ridden horse. He could just see over the mesquite. Diego on the grullo was coming from the Kiowa camp. His straw hat was at his back, held by the rawhide thong around the Mexican's neck. He was crouched over the grullo's withers, using his whip handle as a bat and punching the horse's ribs with his big Mexican rowels. The grullo, wild-eyed and foaming at the mouth, thundered. across the creek, through the mesquite, and up the rise. Walk waited.

The horse reached the top of the rise. Then Diego's high, excited voice called the turn:

"*Los soldadas vienen! Los soldados vienen!*" (The soldiers are coming!)

Walk carried the water pail up out of the draw. He looked to the east but saw no soldiers. The Kiowa camp, however, was already in a state of precipitate flight, with tents down or coming down, ponies being loaded, and some already strung out across the Plains toward the northwest.

Walk ascended the rise without hurrying. Then he stopped to stare. The comanchero camp also was a mass of frenzied activity. Already some of the traders were streaming across the Plains to the south and southwest. Others were running across the draw for saddle stock. Ramón and Diego came on the run from the direction of the red cliff. Ramón vaulted into the saddle of the grullo and Diego climbed up behind him. They headed the horse southeast, and Walk concluded their stock was in that direction, for he was sure Ramón would take the blue roan with him.

Estacado was emerging from the taller mesquite with an armful of roots and the grubbing hoe on his shoulder. He grinned as they met near Ramón's wagon. "Might' near unanimous, ain't it?" he asked.

Walk smiled as he looked over the prairie covered with fleeing dark forms of men and horses. "I reckon," he said, "they don't feel up to meeting the Army."

They started toward the wagon. "One thing about it," said Walk. "We probably got rid of Quita. If she's like most Indians, she'll run from the Army on general principles."

But Quita was not gone. They rounded the tailboard of the wagon, and she was standing by the fire. Her eyes were large as they looked toward Walk. Her bronze face was ash-gray; she stirred the boiling clothes automatically.

CHAPTER 12

WALK TOOK QUITA'S FRIGHT FOR GRANTED; INDIANS were always afraid of the Army. Then too, Quita had had no horse, and no person on foot could count on getting far across the Plains alone.

She stirred the clothes with the peeled stick, her large

brown eyes mostly on Walk.

"You want this water in there now?" he asked.

She nodded without speaking.

He poured the water into the big kettle, and Estacado added mesquite roots to the fire around it while Quita continued to poke the clothes. Then Walk and Estacado made a tour of the street.

Mucha Que was completely deserted. There was a haunch of buffalo still being barbecued over a fire; there was an old patched-up bull harness laid out on the ground alongside a *carreta* for repair; the back axle of a Conestoga wagon was blocked up on a rickrack of doubletrees while the wheel, with a new whittled-out rim section in place, lay at one side, and the iron rim lay in a circular fire of glowing coals. Everywhere the comancheros had dropped what they were doing and had run. Walk and Estacado stopped at the end of the street near Ramón's wagon.

"I don't see no dust," said Estacado, with the brim of his shapeless hat pulled low over his eyes as he studied the eastern horizon.

"I don't either," said Walk after a moment of scrutiny. "Sometimes," he observed, "the Indians don't see much difference in one mile and twenty miles when soldiers are coming—especially if they've been trading in something illegal. I reckon that goes for the comancheros too.

"A feller might almost figger they were guilty of something," Estacado observed dryly.

Walk looked at him. "He might if he was a suspicious gent," he agreed.

They went back. Quita was still stirring the kettle-full of clothes. Walk got his rifle, threw out the shells, and set to work swabbing it out with a ramrod. Estacado crawled under the wagon, into the shade, and lay down flat on his back with his hat over his face to keep off the blueflies, and went to sleep. From time to time a high-pitched yell floated into camp from far away as the comancheros herded or stampeded their stock toward the south and west.

After a while Quita fished out a wad of steaming wet clothes with the stick and laid them on the wagon tongue. She got all the clothes out, and then, using the hem of her buckskin skirt to keep from burning her hands, took hold of the bail of the kettle and tried to lift it. It moved, but it was heavy. She got a better hold. Then Walk pushed her aside and pulled the gloves from his hip-pocket. He took the kettle from the fire, carried it off a few yards, and poured out the soapy water. Then he took it down to the creek to wash it out with sand. Quita followed him silently with the clothes, her eyes still large and fearful. He watched her rinse them in the running water, leaving milky swirls in the stream, and he waited while she spread them out on the tops of the mesquite bushes to dry. There were half a dozen red bandanna handkerchiefs, three faded collar-band shirts, half a dozen pairs of socks, and four suits of long underwear—two of white cotton for Walk and two of red flannel for Estacado.

She started back. Walk got the kettle half full of water and carried it beside her. "Why didn't you leave with the others?" he asked.

"I have no horse—nowhere to go, *señor*."

They had dinner some time before noon, and then Quita put on the kettle of water for soup. By early afternoon Walk picked out a small dust cloud on the horizon in the east, and called Estacado. They studied it.

"It's movin' fast and straight," said Estacado.

132

"Prob'ly men on horseback. And from the way it sticks together in a tight cloud, I'd say soldiers. Injuns gener'ly string out a little."

"That looks right to me," said Walk.

"It's a pretty small party, though."

"It's probably only an advance element for the main troops: I suppose they figger they'd like to get up here before the comancheros find out they're on the way and hide all the evidence."

Estacado snorted. Then he said curiously, "Why do you reckon the comancheros were so quick to go off and leave their stuff?"

Walk was thoughtful. "Maybe because they haven't got any money in the stuff anyway—if some white man somewhere is putting up the capital. I suppose there are some here trading on their own, but they'd be stampeded by the rest."

Within a couple of hours they picked out three cavalrymen in blue uniforms, and one civilian. Walk and Estacado went back to their wagon and sat around the simmering soup kettle with Quita. "There's no need to gallivant out there and hang out a welcome sign," said Walk. "The Army knows they aren't wanted in a place like this, and if we acted too hospitable they'd be suspicious."

Quita said nothing, but sat back a way, with her eyes strangely fastened on Walk.

"What's eatin' her?" Estacado asked in a low voice.

Walk answered carelessly, "She doesn't want to go back. She, likes it out here."

They sat around the fire, with the hot sun burning down on their shoulders and backs, and with the steady, strong wind from the west carrying a little dust. Occasionally a drop of juice from the second antelope

133

ham sizzled in the fire. The prairie-dog soup was simmering, and the aroma that came from its surface was about the most delicious food odor Walk had ever smelled. Walk sat on his spurs. Estacado sat cross-legged, Indian-fashion. Quita sat with her legs modestly hidden under her skirt. They heard the soldiers trot up the rise and slow down to a walk, then reach the end of the streets and come to a stop. They heard muttered exclamations, and Estacado said excitedly, "There's a lady's voice."

Walk nodded. "Like as not they've got women running the Army now, the way they're running the Yellowhouse."

A man's voice called, "Hello, hello. Anybody home?"

Walk started to get up, but he heard the horses come his way at a trot and sat down again. The horses approached. When they were about up to his wagon, he swung up easily to his full height, turned on one heel— and looked into the russet eyes of Madeline Hamilton on the rangy bay.

He swept off his tall hat and made an awkward bow. "It's nice to see you, ma'am. I didn't expect a return visit so soon." Then, as he remembered her attempt to whip him, an imp of perverseness got hold of him. She was so refreshingly lovely. Her dark brown hair shimmered in deep red lights, and her brown eyes were like velvet. She was so sure of herself—and so lovely. He noted the gun belt at her slender waist, and said: "Looks like a right nice horse you're ridin', ma'am. Reckon he'd make a good ropin' horse?"

She blushed, and his opinion of her underwent an upward revision, though what on earth she was doing there with the Army he did not know.

An officer pushed forward. He wore a coat of dark blue with yellow facings on the collar, sky-blue trousers with yellow stripes down the sides, and a campaign hat with crossed sabers on the front. He was big and husky and sandy-haired, and his skin was white, but his face and the backs of his hands were covered with large, irregular freckles. He demanded, "Who's the leader of this camp?"

"Ramón, I reckon," Walk said cautiously.

"Ramón who?" the officer snapped.

Walk put his hat on and shook his head. "That I can't tell you. I don't rightly know."

"Where is he now?"

Walk looked blank. He didn't like the officer's arrogance. "I don't know that either."

"What's your name?" the officer demanded.

"Walk Freeman."

"Got a license to trade?" the officer asked brusquely.

Walk said stiffly, "Yes," but made no move to produce it.

"Let's see it."

Walk asked, "Have you got a right to demand it?"

Perhaps because he was young and perhaps because he was officiating before a very attractive young woman, the officer's freckle-splotched face began to turn red with anger.

"Why do you think I'm asking? You comancheros are a bunch of outlaws," he said, and added righteously, "Your actions show it."

"That kind of charge would have to be proved in court, I reckon."

The officer steadied himself. "Why don't you show your license?"

"Because I don't know if you're entitled to demand

135

it.' "

"It says right on there, 'Holder of this permit will exhibit it to proper authorities on demand.' "

"I read that," Walk said quietly.

The officer began to tighten up. His two aides closed up on each side; they were in Army blues, but instead of campaign hats they wore caps that were squashed down toward the front. Madeline Hamilton moved out of the line of fire. Estacado got to his feet and dusted his pants. Quita remained motionless where she sat.

The officer leaned over his horse's neck and said, "You know an Army uniform when you see one, don't you?"

Walk nodded, watching the two men at the officer's rear. The right one, the corporal, was an old-timer, and didn't seem to be unduly excited. The left one was a green private, and might have a nervous trigger finger. Walk wasn't worried about the officer, because the officer knew the law. He would never try to shoot down a white man before witnesses without provocation. But still Walk didn't like his manner.

Walk said: "I sure do. You're wearin' one."

"Then don't you assume I am an officer?"

"I don't assume nothin'," Walk said bluntly. "This ain't an assumin' country. If you see a buck antelope's horns above the grass, you don't assume there's an antelope under them, because it might be a Comanche." He felt suddenly annoyed. "You asked me my name and I told you, but you didn't tell me yours. For your information, that isn't the way we do things out here. Until you tell me who you are, I'm not assumin' anything and I'm not showin' you my license—and you better warn that tenderfoot back there to keep his hand away from his pistol. Men have developed bad hearts

136

foolin' around with hardware at the wrong time."

The officer took a deep breath. He shot a warning glance at the private. He looked back at Walk and swallowed hard. "All right. I'm Lieutenant Robinson of the Eleventh Cavalry. I want to see your permit."

Walk fished a worn, folded piece of paper out of the upper right pocket of his wildcat vest. He unfolded it. The lieutenant was dismounting. He poked the reins at Walk and said, "Here. Hold my horse."

Walk stiffened again. He didn't take the reins. The lieutenant glared at him. Walk said: "You got lots of manners to learn. Back East you maybe had a servant to hold your horse for you. Out here there aren't any servants. A man holds his own horse or turns him loose."

For a moment the lieutenant seemed about to split a saddle girth. Then he cooled off a little. He clamped the reins under his arm. He scanned the permit. "Fort Griffin," he noted, and glanced sharply at Walk. "You come from the east?"

Walk nodded.

"How'd you get over the Caprock with that wagon?"

"I pulled it up with a rope."

The lieutenant looked sour. "You expect me to believe that?"

"My expectations don't count," Walk said. "You asked me a question. I answered it." He glanced at Madeline, and saw her eying the lieutenant and about to speak. He shook his head once, briefly. Let the officer find out for himself; then he'd be easier to get along with.

"It looks to me like your permit is a forgery—and if so, that's one count against you."

"All right," said Walk, "but I want it back."

Robinson gave it back to him. "Where has everybody else gone?"

"That," Walk said truthfully, "is a question I can't answer."

"They were warned, weren't they?"

"Might be. I was down in the draw."

"You saw them take out, didn't you?"

Walk nodded. "For a fact. But they didn't leave no forwarding address."

The lieutenant swung back into the saddle and wheeled his horse. "Search the camp!" he ordered the two troopers. They dismounted and started up the street, looking between and around the wagons. "Maybe there's others here who pick their times to keep their mouths shut," the lieutenant said sourly as he rode off.

Walk turned to Madeline Hamilton. "It ain't much of an outfit, ma'am, but I'd be happy to have you light and sit a while."

She looked at Quita and then at him. Her voice was unexpectedly cold. "No, thank you, Mr. Freeman," she said. She wheeled the bay and rode after Robinson, who was pacing his troopers up the street.

Estacado muttered, "You made yourself a right nice friend out of that lieutenant. He'd hobble your throat with green rawhide if he ever gets a chance."

"He won't get a chance," Walk said with assurance. "He's an Easterner," he added, "and he needs to learn some manners. When he does that, he'll be all right." He watched them down the street. "What got into the lady from the Yellowhouse?"

Estacado scratched his bushy head and shook it slowly. "Can't say as I know, Walk. When she first laid eyes on you she durn' near melted down an' dropped off her saddle like tallow in a hot sun, but right now one look from her would give a rattlesnake a bellyache. That there lady is changeable as the Pecos River in the spring."

In a few minutes the lieutenant came trotting back with Madeline at his side. "Now look here," he started off angrily, "you can't run circles around me like this. I want to know why everybody is gone from this camp."

Walk rose again to his full height. His tall hat added another foot. He was lean and weather-tanned, and his eyes were beginning to narrow. "You found *me* here, didn't you?"

The lieutenant saw which way it was going, and flushed again.

Walk went on unhurriedly. "I can't answer for the rest, but I can answer for me when you quit playing Army and ask me a reasonable question. There's no way I could know why everybody left. It could be they knew you were coming—and I reckon there's no law against going out to pick daisies whenever a man pleases."

"This is rebel country," the lieutenant began harshly. "You can't—"

"It ain't rebel country," Walk said. "Texas has been readmitted to the Union.

The lieutenant got control of himself again. "All right," he said. "You're calling the turns—but you'd better be in the clear, Freeman. If I get a chance to hang anything on you, it'll be on your neck. There've been complaints from all over West Texas and half of New Mexico about the comancheros, and I've got orders to cleanup the trade."

"What's dirty about it?" asked Walk.

"The comancheros are trading guns and ammunition. There was a new law on that last spring, and I'm going to enforce it."

"The new law," Walk said, "provides that the superintendent of an Indian agency can revoke a license to trade *if* he figgers he ought to."

The lieutenant stiffened. "A Plains lawyer, eh?"

"I looked up those things before I come out here," Walk said modestly.

"You're stretchin' your neck," the lieutenant warned him.

Walk nodded confidently. "Nobody else has stretched it yet." He asked, "You got any proof the Indians been stealin' critters from the ranchmen?"

"Plenty of it. Miss Hamilton here lost her favorite saddle horse in an Indian raid about a month ago."

Walk turned his calm gay eyes on Madeline. He lifted his hat a little. "What kind of horse was it, ma'am?"

For the first time she spoke to him kindly, even hopefully. "A blue roan stallion with the Tres Casas on the right hip," she said.

Walk paused. He moistened his lips with his tongue. He looked at Madeline Hamilton. Her rich brown hair showed a deep auburn, and her eyes were a vivid russet that reflected sparks like tiny particles of silver dropping through water in the sunlight. Walk opened his mouth, then closed it.

"I'm sorry, ma'am," he said finally. "I reckon it isn't in *my* string."

He saw the hope die in her eyes, and he felt like a mangy coyote.

CHAPTER 13

"THE THEFT OF STOCK AND TRADING TO THE comancheros has become a regular traffic," the lieutenant complained.

"Looks to me," Walk said, like it's time for the ranchmen to get together. If Colorado cattlemen would recognize Texas brands, and the other way around, there wouldn't be any market for stolen cattle."

The lieutenant answered, "I'm not here to argue economics. President Grant has been raising holy Ned with General Augur of the Military Department of Texas. The comancheros are violating the treaty of 1846 by supplying whisky to the Comanches; then the Indians go on the warpath and innocent citizens get killed. Have you thought of that?"

Walk nodded soberly. "I know it."

"All these things—whisky, arms, and ammunition, stealing and murdering—have their origin in the comanchero trade."

"I doubt that," Walk said. "I figger some of it goes back to Texas cattlemen looking for grass, and some of it goes back to plain cussedness on the part of the Indians. It isn't all the fault of the comancheros."

Robinson glanced at him. "The general has given us orders to straighten out this business or wipe the comancheros off the Plains."

Walk looked at Madeline Hamilton and did not quite restrain a smile at Robinson's melodramatic words. "Have your cattle been taken, Miss Hamilton?"

"All summer," she said. "Every time the moon was full. Three nights ago there was a raid, and they got

141

sixteen head of three- and four-year-old steers."

"The Indians have been hungry, ma'am. There aren't many buffalo on the Plains."

"They don't steal for food," she said. "They trade the stock for guns and whisky. That definitely puts the blame on the comancheros."

Walk smiled wistfully. "You seem right set against us traders, ma'am."

She looked over his head.

Robinson dismounted abruptly, as though impatient with the interruption. There wasn't much cantle on his Army saddle, and he slid down very smartly. "I must admit," he said with sarcasm, "that I am not a student of causes and effects. I'm an Army man, and I've been sent to do a job. Now you, Freeman—have you been trading for cattle?"

"It's an insult to a self-respecting longhorn steer to call them cattle," Walk said, "but you're welcome to look 'em over. They're about four miles off to the southwest there—all twelve of 'em—and one slick-eared broomtail."

Robinson tied his horse's reins to Walk's front wheel.

"I hope that Army horse will stay where he's tied," Walk said. "If he don't, the government is going to owe me for a wagon wheel."

Robinson glared at Walk, spun an his heel, and went down the street. Madeline Hamilton, stony-faced, rode slowly out to the south and sat her horse, scanning the flat prairie. Walk watched her and sighed softly.

Estacado said, "He didn't answer you."

Walk said soberly, "I reckon I've provoked him enough."

"I figger you provoked him away *too* much."

"He rubs me wrong," Walk said.

142

"All the same, he's the law on the Plains—what there is—and I never aimed to cross the law too far."

"I brought no whisky," Walk said, "and I brought no arms or ammunition to trade. The most he can say is that I traded for some stock with brands I didn't know." Walk took a deep breath. "I fought in the Rebellion before I was weaned, and I've paid plenty for it, but in the eyes of the law I'm a citizen. They gave us back the right to vote and carry on affairs the same as before. 'Hold my horse' he said!" Walk took a deep breath. "For six years I was manhandled by carpetbagger courts supported by this same Army, and I figured when I came out here I could start over fair and square."

"He's only doin' his job the best he knows how." Estacado looked worried. "Are you aimin' to fight the Rebellion all over again?"

"They sure haven't been very friendly to us since we hit the Yellowhouse," Walk said slowly. "I guess it kind of got under my hide."

Estacado frowned until his eyes almost disappeared in his black-bearded face. "I know how you feel about it, but I been around a long time, and I found out that just about the time a feller gits to feelin' his oats and rubs it into the other gent more'n what he might, he's generally heading straight into a box canyon."

"Don't worry," Walk advised. "I'm laying off him from now on."

"You've already talked loud enough to make every officer in the U.S. Army mad at you."

"Stir the soup," Walk said.

But Quita pushed the old mountain man back. "Sit down, Chief. I cook soup. You rest."

Estacado walked out into the street mumbling. Then he straightened. "They're starting to search the

143

wagons," he said.

Walk watched the corporal and the private go to the rear end of the first wagon across the street. Walk and Estacado stood out behind, watching. The troopers pulled out a big bale of buffalo robes, and Walk grunted.

"What do you reckon they'll find?" asked Estacado.

Walk said thoughtfully, "Nothing."

"Then why did the comancheros run?"

"Might be several reasons. Take a fellow like Batty Simpkins; he doesn't want to meet the law. A few like him light out, and the rest follow before they get their thinking caps on straight." He frowned as one of the troopers vaulted into the wagon and shoved out a heavy packing case. The other soldier held onto it until the first one jumped down. They lifted it to the ground together, and one of them began to knock off the top boards with a hatchet head. "There's nothing illegal about buying stock from the Indians as long as you paid for it; all they can do is take it away from you." He watched them open the case and take out small boxes that, when opened, revealed strings of colored glass beads. "There *is* something wrong," he said slowly. "Ramón knows all those things. Why did *he* run?"

The soldiers opened another case. It was filled with small buckets of green paint.

"Comanche war paint," Walk observed. "But that isn't against the law either."

Estacado looked up. "It makes it easier for the Comanches to go on the warpath."

"They don't need anything to make it easier."

There was an open box with bread wrapped in newspapers, and several boxes of soda crackers. Then there was an exclamation from one of the soldiers, and he came to the tailboard with a gallon jug of wine, half empty.

The lieutenant looked at it and swore. Walk grinned. "Even an Army officer doesn't have to be kicked in the pants with a red-hot branding iron to know that's personal drinking liquor."

Estacado watched it thirstily. "You don't s'pose he's gonna pour it out?"

"I don't think so. Keep an eye on it. We'll need something to drown our tears when Robinson leaves."

Quita's soft voice said, "The soup is ready, *señores*."

Walk started back to the fire. Then he looked toward Madeline Hamilton, still sitting her horse aloofly, watching the men search the camp, occasionally scanning the prairie. In long strides he reached her side. He stretched one arm and put his hand on the cantle behind her, and the other on the saddle horn. She wasn't very big, and he didn't have to look up far to smile at her. "We're just havin' supper, ma'am. I'd be pleased to have you eat with us."

She looked over his head toward Estacado and Quita and the kettle of soup, then back at him, and said stiffly, "No, thank you, Mr. Freeman." She added: "You have done well in the short time you have been here. The Indian girl is very pretty."

Her horse started to move off, and Walk let her go. The bay moved slowly to the north, and Walk took a step toward her, but stopped. He could not explain Quita, for that would bring up the fact that he had had the blue roan, and it would be harder to explain why he traded away the horse than it would be to clarify Quita's position. He went slowly to the camp.

Estacado was drinking soup. He looked at Walk over the edge of the tin cup. Walk said briefly, "I reckon some people's taste doesn't run to prairie dogs."

Estacado asked, "How'd she know it was prairie-dog soup?"

Walk was sitting on his spurs. He looked up, abashed. "Come to think about it, she didn't."

Quita, dipping up a cupful of steaming hot soup, held it over the kettle a moment to drip, and looked at Walk. "Is the *señorita* you weesh to marry?"

"That's the lady I had in mind," Walk admitted, "but I'm beginnin' to wonder if maybe I aimed at somethin' so good it's not worth having."

"Is a nice lady," said Quita, and handed him the cup. "*Es muy simpática.*"

The soup smelled good and tasted better. Walk had six cupfuls. "You're a good cook, Quita."

She gave him a brief, grateful smile. "Thank you, *señor.*"

Walk rocked to his feet. "The U.S. Army is getting along with its housecleaning."

The soldiers were nearing the end of the street. The last cart produced eight or ten bolts of vivid calicos and two worn tablecloths filled with bread and tied with knots over the top. They tossed the stuff back in the cart and went to Ramón's wagon at the head of Walk's side of the street.

Walk observed to Estacado: "He won't find a thing he can complain about. All the comancheros in with Ramón undoubtedly keep their liquor and guns stashed away in his hideout; and he was probably tipped off by the gent who's running this thing that the Army was liable to get in on the play."

"I figger everybody is in with Ramón but us."

"Personally, I don't like to be staked out with such a short picket rope, but some people aren't so fussy," said

Walk.

They watched the soldiers come down the line toward them, digging out beads, paint, knives, calico, trinkets covered with tinsel, Spanish-type combs and earbobs, a swallowtail coat, an old silk hat, Mother Hubbards, cheap tarpaulins, an ornate British Army coat from the War of 1812, candles, smoking and chewing tobacco and snuff, and cheap, gaily colored handkerchiefs. "Mighty near ev'rything," Walk observed, "but pants. Not even a comanchero can trade pants to an Indian."

The soldiers finished the cart next to Walk's wagon. Lieutenant Robinson glared at Walk; Robinson was tired and dirty and disgruntled, and probably hungry.

"I reckon," Walk said, "since my wagon is my home, you haven't got a right to search it as long as I object."

Robinson said acidulously, "You've been reading a book."

"I'm going to do you a favor, Lieutenant," said Walk. "To keep you from making an eight-hundred-mile trip to Gainesville and back for a search warrant, and to clear myself, I'm giving you permission to search my wagon."

He thought he heard a choked gasp behind him, and Robinson looked over his shoulder, but Walk kept his eye on the lieutenant.

"You mean that?" Robinson asked suspiciously.

"I mean it."

"If I find anything," Robinson warned, "it will be legal evidence against you."

"You're in the saddle," Walk said. "Let's see if you can ride."

Robinson barked at his men, "Pull the stuff out of there."

The two soldiers moved to the tailboard and slid out

147

an open box. They placed it on the ground and unpacked it. The contents were all thin cardboard boxes of sacked tobacco.

The second box was a big case filled with bolts of cloth. They took out all the cloth and emptied the box to the bottom, then put it all back in.

They wrestled out the hogshead filled with pones of *cemita* wrapped in newspapers. They looked at the lieutenant. He took hold of one edge of the barrel and tilted it; he tried it from the other edge. Then he shook his head. "Nothing there," he said. They threw the tarp back and went farther. Out came a slat-sided box filled with tin pie plates. Another held nested rings of tin cups tied together with baling wire.

There was the box of small bottles of cheap perfume. Robinson looked at Walk. Walk shrugged. Robinson opened one bottle and sniffed. He tasted it and made a face. "Not even a Comanche would drink that stuff," he said.

Walk grinned.

They took out the apple box filled with cooking implements, and the two grubbing hoes. The two men climbed back into the wagon.

The box of alarm clocks was next, and Walk watched, amused. But they didn't slide it back. They were taking a small tarp from something beside it. Walk frowned. He hadn't had any tarps under the big one. But before he could figure anything out, the private yelled: "We got it, sir! We got it!"

Robinson glanced at Walk. He looked puzzled, as if he were expecting some kind of trick, but when he saw Walk's open mouth he showed a satisfied smile. "Leave it on the tailboard, boys."

They set a small five-gallon keg on one end.

Robinson approached the keg. He walked around it. Then he turned the wooden spigot a little while he held his fingers under it. A few drops of a sour-smelling amber liquid dripped over his fingers. He sniffed them and tasted the liquid. Then he wheeled triumphantly on Walk. "All right, comanchero, you're under arrest." His pistol was in his hand. "The charge is possession of five gallons of bourbon whisky for illegal trading with the Indians."

Walk was stunned. He stared into the wagon. Nothing was left but his rifle and the cowhide and the box of alarm clocks. He turned on the spigot and let the liquid drip on on his own fingers. He smelled it and tasted it. Then he looked at Robinson. "That's not bourbon," he said. "That's rye."

"Back up to me," Robinson ordered.

Walk turned slowly. Robinson lifted Walk's .44 out of his holster. "Corporal," he said, "heave his stuff back in there. Get that rifle and any other arms you can find, and guard these two men until the troop gets here."

Grim rather than triumphant, he spoke to Walk. "I see your game now. You figured I was going to search you anyway, and you tried to bluff by offering to permit it. You thought I'd refuse. I called your bluff, mister, and I'm warning you: don't, try to meet my play!"

CHAPTER 14

TWO BUCK-SKINNED, LONG-HAIRED SCOUTS APPEARED over the rise, one on each side of the draw, about a quarter of a mile apart, riding easily. There were far-carrying, leather-lunged commands. Then the cavalry broke over the rise in a column of two's. They made a nice sight, dressed in blue uniforms with accordion-like caps squashed down in front, all heads up, all elbows close in to their bodies, all riding erect. Sabers clanked, leather creaked, hooves clopped rhythmically. They were led by a sergeant who rode easily and militarily on a big bay horse. Behind him the guidon sergeant had broken out a split-tailed red-and-white pennant with an *E* on it as the troop designation, and beside the guidon sergeant was a soldier bearing the regimental flag of the Eleventh Cavalry.

The column of two's curved over the rise and came toward camp. Robinson mounted his own horse and rode down the street to meet them before the camp. Behind the troopers came two prairie wagons, high and narrow, each pulled by a four-horse team. These came over the rise at a trot also, and the wind caught them and billowed out the canvas on the bowed hoops.

"Right purty sight," said Estacado.

Walk nodded. "That's what scared the lobo back on the Plains this morning," he observed.

Estacado looked thoughtful. "You reckon they scared off the Comanches too? Quita said they'd be here today."

"I don't know, but Quita probably knew what she was talking about."

"This here's a nice outfit," Estacado observed.

Walk nodded. "Every piece of leather in the troop has been saddle-soaped—bridles, halters, reins, saddles, boots, belts, and harness."

Estacado grunted. "Every piece of brass and nickel has been polished too," he noted. "I'd hate to think how far the light would reflect off of one of them Army spurs. I bet the Indians could see that outfit from here to Fort Sumner."

"They'll learn," said Walk. "Robinson's no fool. Look at those horses. Any man who can bring a big outfit across the Plains in a summer like this and keep them like that is smart enough to get by anywhere."

The sergeant raised his arm. The column came to a neat halt before Robinson.

Estacado nudged Walk vigorously. "Was that one little whiff too much for you," he asked, "or do you see what I see?"

Walk said, puzzled, "They've captured Ramón and Diego."

"Sir," the sergeant said to Robinson, "we have taken two prisoners who admit they are from this camp."

Estacado whispered hoarsely, "I smell polecat. Ramón left camp on the black. Now he's riding the blue roan stallion."

Walk nodded and watched intently. Ramón, with his swarthy face shaded by his square-topped, shaggy hat with the thongs under his chin, and with the green sash around his waist, rode up to the front, accompanied by the wizened little Diego in the huge straw hat, and followed closely by a soldier. Ramón seemed different in some way Walk could not quite put his finger on. His dark face was marked with red spots and blisters where Quita's coals had hit him. Neither of the two seemed concerned at being caught.

Walk said quietly, "There's dead turtle around here, all right. With a million miles of prairie to get lost in, and a horse like that to ride, how did those two sidewinders ever manage to walk into the hands of the Army?"

"And why"

"It's a cinch," Walk observed, "that he knows about that whisky in my wagon."

151

"But that ain't why he came back," said Estacado. "He didn't need to come back for that. Whatever he come back for hasn't showed up yet."

Walk shifted his red bandanna on his neck and looked down at Estacado without enthusiasm. "What are you drivin' at, Estacado Smith?"

"Somebody don't want you in Mucha Que, and this is a good way to get rid of you and clear themselves at the same time. They're out to plant you, and that's why they came back. It isn't just that keg they stashed in your wagon." Estacado took a deep breath. "There's more comin', Walk. Brace yourself."

Walk pulled his tall hat down tight. "You don't mind if we go up a little closer?" he asked the corporal.

"I guess not. Just don't try anything," the corporal said.

The first sergeant was a grizzled campaigner. He was saying, "It looks strange to me, sir, that these two men let themselves be captured."

Ramón grinned.

"You never saw better teeth on a three-year-old," Estacado said witheringly.

Robinson was riding around the two captives. He went all the way around at a walk, while Ramón seemed to hunch his shoulders a little. Finally the lieutenant was back in front. He wheeled his horse and faced Ramón. "That blue roan," he said, "is a mighty nice animal."

Ramón grinned again. He tried to make it seem feeble, and Walk began to see the drift, "*Sí, señor,*" Ramón said. "*Muy bonito*—very pretty."

"A blue roan," the lieutenant said. "There aren't many of those on the Plains."

"*No, señor. No hay muchos.*"

Estacado whispered, "If I ever seen a picture of a man

trying to act guilty when he figgers he ain't, this is it."

Walk's jaws tightened.

"Also," said Robinson, "there are mighty few blue roans on the Plains with a Tres Casas brand on the right hip."

Ramón was the picture of exaggerated unhappiness. *"No, señor."*

Estacado nudged Walk again. "There's the Yellowhouse filly coming up behind Ramón's wagon."

Walk took a deep breath and nodded.

Robinson turned to the sergeant. "Jenkins, take the troop up above this camp. The scouts will help you find uncontaminated water. Send out two foraging parties, one scout with each party. We can probably find plenty of mesquite wood along the draw, but send out a couple of parties to both sides to see if they can scare up some game. Make camp and report to me. Take care of the horses and tell the mess sergeant to feed the men as soon as he can."

"Yes, sir."

"Leave these two greasers here with a couple of men to guard them."

"Yes, sir." The sergeant wheeled his horse and took his place at the head of the column. "Forwa-ard . . ." He made a fist of his right hand and pumped it a couple of times at the sky. The column broke into a walk. The sergeant led them around the camp to keep out of the mesquite. Their blue uniforms and caps were very neat in the last rays of the sun.

Madeline Hamilton came around the last wagon and uttered a little cry. "That's my horse!"

"Yes, ma'am," said Robinson. "You can have him in a minute. I got some questions to ask first."

Walk and Estacado were standing at the front of

Ramón's wagon. Walk put one booted foot up on the wagon tongue.

Robinson said to Ramón, "You stole that horse."

The half-breed shook his head with wide swings. "*No, señor*, I do not steal him."

"Where'd you get him, then?"

Ramón pointed over Robinson's shoulder at Walk Freeman. "I trade from him. It's his horse, but we trade."

Walk heard a gasp, but he didn't look at Madeline. Robinson frowned. There was movement back of the wagon. Walk whispered to Estacado, "You got a prairie-dog hole handy?"

"Sorry, son, mine is full up," Estacado said, pulling his old hat lower over his eyes.

Madeline Hamilton stepped her bay around the wagon and confronted Walk. Her russet eyes blazed with indignation and fury. "You had him—and you knew he was mine, because I told you about him down in the Yellowhouse. You had him and you traded him off to this Mexican."

"Yes, ma'am," Walk said miserably.

"I asked you a while ago," she went on relentlessly, "and you lied to me."

Walk swallowed. "No, ma'am. I told you he wasn't in my string."

Her face was filled with scorn, and her lips curled in loathing. "Liar!" she said. The word was scorching. "Horse thief!"

"Ma'am," he said reproachfully, "those are strong words."

Her curled lips straightened a little. "You could have told me," she said.

Robinson said, "It begins to look as if maybe you did

154

come up the Yellowhouse after all—but it also begins to look as if I got the king bee around here the first swipe. You might even be the man behind the comancheros, Freeman—the one who puts up the money and the one who tips off the Indians where to raid."

"I might be," Walk said, "but I'm not."

The corporal guarding Walk spoke up. "Sir, there is a cowhide in the wagon, and there seems to be quite a bit of money in it."

Ramón's eyes dilated at the mention of money. But Robinson looked unexpectedly grim. "We'll go have a look, corporal."

He led the way. He dismounted and tied his horse to the front wagon wheel. The corporal and the private got in the wagon and wrestled the cowhide bundle to the tailboard. They jumped down and slid it to the ground.

"Open it up," said Robinson.

They tried, but the knots on top were like molded iron. Walk said nothing as they skinned knuckles and broke fingernails.

"How do you get it open?" Robinson demanded of Walk.

"I'll tell you," Walk said, "but first I want to go on record. There's 2,500 dollars in silver pesos in that hide, and if I lose it on account of this, I'll put in a claim to the government."

"Pesos? You mean Mexican money?"

"That's what I mean."

"How many laws can you violate at once? Mexican money isn't legal tender in the United States."

Walk said laconically, "It may not be legal tender in the United States, but down here in the Southwest it'll buy more than any other kind of money."

Robinson's face tightened up. "You're laying

yourself open to a charge of smuggling."

"I'll answer that at the proper time," Walk said.

Robinson sneered. "No doubt the answer will be good."

"It will be."

"All right. How do you get it open?"

Walk said, "Give me a grubbing hoe."

Robinson nodded at the corporal. The soldier handed him the heavy cross-bladed implement. Walk glanced up at Robinson. The lieutenant had his right hand on the butt of his pistol. Walk raised the hoe carefully and took a swing. The sharp, heavy blade sheared through the knots, and most of them disappeared. He took another swing, then laid the grubbing hoe on the tailboard, and stepped back. "You can pull it apart now," he said.

The two men pulled the sides apart, as if opening up a folded flower. As the cowhide yielded stiffly, Robinson swallowed audibly at the sight of half a bushel of silver pesos, flowing together like wheat in a bin, clinking softly as they changed position and the pile flattened out with the expanding sides of the container.

Ramón's eyes glittered. He met Walk's glance, and for an instant there was implacable hatred in his swarthy, redsplotched face. The half-breed hadn't dreamed that Walk had had that silver; if he had, he would have taken steps to get it, but now it was too late—or was it?

"Count it into that leather bucket," Robinson told the corporal, and turned to Walk. "Mr. Freeman, where did a comanchero trader get 2,500 silver pesos?"

"In San Antone," Walk said.

"What did you intend to do with all this money, if not to finance the other traders?"

For the first time Walk's dream sounded crazy even

to himself. "I brought it," he said, "to start a ranch on the Plains."

Robinson snorted. "Nobody in his right mind would ever start a ranch up here on this desert. Where did you get that stallion?" he asked suddenly.

Walk said, "I bought it from an Indian."

"What Indian?"

Walk didn't answer.

"How do I know you didn't steal this horse yourself?"

Walk said quietly, "Miss Hamilton told me the blue roan was missing when I came up the Yellowhouse canyon, and I sure didn't have him then."

Robinson turned to Ramón. "Do you know the name of the Indian he bought the roan from?"

Ramón smiled profusely. *"No, señor."* He shrugged his shoulders under Robinson's stare. "I know nothing. I trade the horse from thees fellow."

Robinson looked at Walk again.

"Indians all look alike to me," Walk said. "I never asked his name."

"Then I'm going to charge you with horse stealing, and you can see what the judge back in Gainesville thinks about your story."

Walk remained silent. He avoided Madeline Hamilton's eyes. But Quita's clear soft voice floated out from somewhere behind him. "He trade' the horse from an Indian," she said. "I see."

Robinson swung on Quita. "What tribe?" he asked.

"Kiowa."

Walk did not look around at Quita.

"What name?"

"Flying Bear."

Robinson said skeptically, "Never heard of him."

Madeline Hamilton's bay moved forward a step as

she leaned over his neck. "Who are you?" she asked, and there was something in her tone that made Walk's face burn.

"I am Quita," the girl said softly.

"Indian?"

"Pah-Ute."

"What are you doing here?"

Quita's voice was proud. "He trade' the horse for me. I am Andale's slave."

Madeline pressed forward. "Whose slave?" she asked.

Walk could feel Quita's finger pointing at his back. "Walk's," she said proudly, and repeated, "I am Andale's slave."

Madeline gasped. Her eyes burned Walk as they touched him.

"Slavery!" Robinson roared. "The Civil War outlawed that." He wheeled on Walk. "Haven't you rebels learned that yet?" His voice was furious with indignation. "This will put you in the penitentiary for the rest of your life—if your own people don't hang you first. Corporal!"

"Yes, sir."

"It is imperative that we get these two men back to Fort Griffin. I will hold you personally responsible."

"Yes, sir."

Walk looked up from the end of the wagon tongue. Robinson's freckle-splotched face was the picture of wrath. Walk turned to Madeline Hamilton. Her lips curled in scorn. He looked at Estacado, but the older man was staring at the ground. Then he looked back at Quita.

Quita's glance was darting from one face to another. She looked at Walk, her eyes fearful. "*Señor!*" she

158

cried. "Have I say something wrong?" Suddenly she was on her knees. "I am only trying to help. It is not right they should take you for horse stealing. You have not steal any horse."

Walk smiled at her and said gently, "You have said nothing wrong, *señorita*—nothing." He added quietly, "You had better see after the clothes. They will be dry by now."

CHAPTER 15

ROBINSON WAS GRIM. HE SAID TO RAMÓN: "GET OFF that blue roan and turn him over to the lady. You can ride double with your sidekick. That way I can watch you better—although I don't think you amount to much around here."

Ramón smiled widely and showed his teeth. He bowed and said, "*Sí, señor, como V. quiere*—as you wish," and dismounted with alacrity. He led the stallion to Madeline Hamilton. He offered her the reins, took off his black hat, and made a sweeping bow. *"Perdóneme, señorita,* I have make a ba-ad mistake." He shrugged and brought his palms up in a liquid movement. "But you no be angry at me, *señorita.* Any man would lose his judgment at such a *caballo simpático.*"

She answered shortly, "It's all right." She was off the bay. She approached the roan. He pranced forward a step and slid his jaw over her shoulder. Her eyes were going over him for signs of abuse.

Ramón backed several steps from her, while Robinson watched him narrowly. "I am only an ignorant *mejicano, señorita.* You weel forgive Ramón—*sí?*" He showed his teeth in a supplicating smile.

159

She nodded without emotion, rubbing the roan's neck with her slim white hands.

Ramón got up behind Diego. Ramón had changed his feathers. He looked fat and helpless, and his face was blank except for the suggestion of a relatively harmless, ingratiating duplicity; he seemed now like a man of small capacity, who had committed crimes, perhaps, but only very small crimes. By focusing attention on that idea, Ramón undoubtedly hoped to avoid scrutiny on more serious charges. Walk snorted, but he knew it might work. Ramón now looked like an egg stealer—not a killer.

And evidently Robinson was deceived. He spoke to one of the men. "Earnshaw, go with Corporal Watkins and guard Freeman. One man will be enough to watch the Mexicans." He turned to the corporal. "Take these two whites back to their wagon and let them get their personal belongings. Don't let them handle anything first. They can point out what they want, and you examine it to be sure there aren't any concealed weapons. Take that silver to camp and put it in a locker in one of the wagons."

"Yes, sir."

Walk and Estacado followed the corporal back to the wagon. Quita's soup was still simmering. "You fellows might as well help yourselves to that," Walk said. "I don't reckon we'll need it."

The corporal's face lighted up. "We'll do that—but don't try anything," he warned.

The lieutenant passed them on the way to the military camp a mile upstream. The sun was down, and soldiers at the camp were grooming their horses on the picket line. Behind Robinson, Ramón and Diego jogged along. The lone guard rode in the rear. Madeline rode

160

alongside Robinson.

The corporal got two tin cups and went to the soup kettle. Walk and Estacado sat on the wagon tongue. Estacado said, "There's some mighty funny business going on here. Ramón's putting on a good show now, but he don't dare go back to Gainesville and testify against you in court. I don't know nothin' about law, but I know when he puts on that helpless Mexican act the judge down in Texas isn't gonna swallow it."

Walk said thoughtfully: "That's the only chance we have, though. We've got to get back to civilization and stand trial in a real court. I can show where I got the silver. I can prove I haven't ever been up here on the Plains before—and that's the main thing that's eating on the lieutenant. They sent him here to clean up the comanchero trade, and they told him they think there's a white man behind it. The lieutenant finds me; I'm white, and he figures I'm the one. He'll throw everything in the book at me to be sure to keep me off the Plains. But it'll be all right," he said confidently, "when we get back to Gainesville before a real court."

"Except for that charge of slavery."

Walk swallowed hard. He had forgotten that.

"Say, that's why Ramón rode the blue roan when he got captured by the Army—to bring up that slavery charge!"

Walk said slowly, "That means somebody mighty smart is behind all this. That was a sharp play."

"Somebody wants you out of the way *bad*. Say, listen—what if you don't get back to stand trial?"

Walk frowned. "Sure I'm going back."

Estacado scratched his head. "I'm beginnin' to make some sense out of this whole deal. Ramón got caught on purpose. Why? *So he could keep an eye on you and be*

161

sure you don't get back!"

"You're talkin' through your hat."

"That's the only thing that adds up around here."

"Ramón's under guard. He wouldn't dare do anything like that."

"It's four hundred miles to Gainesville," Estacado pointed out, "and Ramón will have the run of the camp before we're forty-eight hours on the trail. With all these charges against you, is anybody going to bother too much if you have an accident?"

Walk said slowly through thin lips, "You're talkin' gumption, old-timer. With you and me unarmed and Ramón practically free, all he has to do is wait. He can pick a fight with me, and then Diego will slip in and knife me in the back—and suppose it's night and nobody saw what happened; Ramón claims I was trying to escape." He groaned.

The corporal and the private finished their fourth cup of soup. The corporal patted his stomach. "I don't mind you fellows talking," he said, "but I've got a job to do here. What do you want to take with you?"

Walk looked at him solemnly. "If I had my choice I'd take my .44, but I reckon that's out of the picture. How about my blankets and that small tarp?"

The corporal had the private unroll the blankets and shake them out. He nodded, satisfied.

"That's my saddle on the end gate and my bridle on the post there," said Walk.

"We'll leave them with the wagon. I suppose the lieutenant will take the wagon back if you've got anything to pull it."

"I've got four of the best mules from South Texas."

"When you're talkin' about mules," the corporal said, "there ain't no 'best'."

162

Just then Quita came in from the draw with an armload of dry clothes. "What of me, *señor*? What happen to Quita?"

Walk said, "I'll speak to the lieutenant. He'll probably take you to Fort Griffin and send you back to your tribe—since you're Paiute."

"I not want to go back," she said. "I want stay with you."

Walk sighed. "It's gonna be right crowded with three in one jail cell."

Quita turned away. The corporal said, grinning, "Some little squaw you got there, mister."

Walk spun on his heel so fast the corporal drew his pistol. "She isn't a squaw," Walk said through thin lips. "And if you lay a hand on her, I'll shove your teeth down your throat."

"Careful, mister," the corporal said hastily. "I've got the gun."

"You've got the teeth too," said Walk uncompromisingly.

The lieutenant came up while Walk was tying up his bedroll and his few extra clothes inside the blanket, with his tin plate at one end, and his cup, fork, and spoon tied together with rawhide and fastened under the thongs that bound the blanket.

"You better turn the Indian girl over to the Army," Walk said to the lieutenant. "She was taken by the Apaches and traded to a white man. They'd be glad to get her back, I imagine."

Robinson said: "You're the white man. You ought to know."

Walk stiffened, but Robinson went on. "I'll see she's delivered at Fort Griffin in the same shape she's in now—whatever that is. Can this old duffer drive your

163

wagon?"

"Listen," said Estacado belligerently. "I'm the best mule skinner on the Llano Estacado."

"Then you drive the wagon back."

A man in a blue uniform came loping across the prairie from the south. The soldier came up to Robinson and saluted. "Sir," he said, "we've found a skeleton. The scout says it's a fresh skeleton."

Robinson said sharply, "Of a man?"

"Yes, sir."

Robinson's eyes were bright. "Fresh, eh?"

"Yes, sir. Hext is bringing it in a blanket."

The lieutenant nodded and looked sharply at Walk.

The scout came up carrying something wrapped in the Army blanket, and dismounted gingerly. No one spoke. The man laid the blanket on the ground and slowly unrolled it. Then he stood back.

Although there was no particle of flesh on the bones, they were not the chalk-white of old bones, but had a pinkish tinge that was noticeable even in the growing darkness.

"The head was a couple of hundred yards away," said the soldier.

There was no mistaking the wooden stub attached to one leg below the kneebone. A rawhide harness that had held it in place loosely surrounded the lower thigh bone.

"Coyotes pretty hungry this year," Robinson said.

"It's been a mighty dry year," said Walk.

"You know him?"

Walk nodded slowly. "That's Pegleg Popham."

"Who killed him?"

Walk frowned. "I reckon that there's a question of law."

Robinson's eyes narrowed. He snapped at the

corporal, "Watkins, go back to camp and get that greaser."

"Yes, sir."

Madeline rode up. She avoided Walk's eyes, but when she saw the skeleton she paled a little. Ramón came, riding Diego's grullo slack-muscled and sodden, and grinning like a man of defective mentality.

Robinson said, "Get off that horse."

"*Sí, señor.*" Ramón got down, pretending to be so clumsy that he almost fell off, while Walk watched coldly.

Robinson pointed to the bones laid out on the blanket. "Know who that is?"

Ramón shook his head vigorously. "*No, señor.*"

"You ever see that wooden leg?"

Ramón stared at it. Walk saw a look of cunning cross his eyes. "*Sí*—I have see' it," he said slowly.

"Where?"

"A *tejano*—he came here—two—three—four days it makes now."

"What happened to him?"

Ramón shrugged. "*Yo no sé.*" He was standing on the very spot, Walk noted, where Pegleg's wagon had been burned two nights before.

Robinson glared at Ramón for a moment. Then he turned his scrutiny on Walk. "Pegleg Popham came into Fort Griffin four weeks ago," he said. "He was headed for the Llano Estacado, and he intended to go up on the Caprock through the *puerta* at Las Lenguas. It looks to me like he made it. He reached Mucha Que. But he wasn't here long. What happened to him here? How long have you been here, Freeman?"

"Two days," Walk said.

"You must have seen this man before the coyotes and

165

buzzards got to him. You must know what happened to him."

Walk stared at the bones on the blanket. Ramón would expect to be accused. Walk crossed him up by saying nothing. He wanted time to think.

Robinson swung on Ramón. "Who killed him?"

Ramón shrugged, his eyes wide.

Robinson's hard blue eyes swept the bones. He swung back to Walk. "There's no evidence of a bullet," he said. "That means he likely was knifed. Have you got a knife?"

Walk said slowly, his eyes fixed on Robinson's face, "Do you think I'd come out here without one?"

"Let's see it."

Walk handed him a huge jackknife. The lieutenant pulled open the big blade. He looked at the thumbnail notch. Blood," he announced.

"Antelope," Walk said.

Robinson glared. "Maybe. I'll keep the knife anyway." He looked speculatively at Walk. He tossed the knife up and down in his freckle-splotched hand. "When I saw that keg of whisky in your wagon," he said, "it was funny to me that a man as smart as you would lay yourself open like that. Now," he said slowly, "maybe I'm beginning to see the answer. You just figured you were so strong out here that you could do anything you wanted to do."

Walk began to tighten up.

"When Pegleg Popham came through the fort," Robinson said, "he told us he wasn't headed for Indian country. But he had a bunch of knicknacks that weren't worth anything to ranchers, and it was pretty plain where he was going. He had one keg of whisky in his wagon, and so the morning he went out after his mules

166

we marked that keg." He paused. "If you got his keg, maybe the mark is still on the bottom. It was three X's made with chalk. That way we figured Pegleg wouldn't pay attention if he happened to see it." He paused again. "Maybe you wouldn't either."

Walk began to turn cold.

"Watkins—"

"Yes, sir."

Robinson led the way back to Walk's wagon. They reached the tailboard. The keg was on the ground. Robinson said sharply, "Up-end it!"

Watkins picked it up carefully. He held it horizontally and turned it so they could see the bottom end. Three small X's in white chalk appeared near one rim.

Walk took a deep breath. Robinson nodded. Watkins set down the keg. Robinson turned on Walk and said harshly, "I charge you with murder."

Walk glanced at Ramón. Behind the half-breed's air of innocence was a gloating hatred. Walk looked at Estacado, who shook his head; he tried to speak, but his black beard quivered and he kept still. There was horror on Madeline's face. Walk looked around at Quita. Her big eyes were soft on Walk; she swept Ramón with scorn, and turned to Robinson. She started to speak, but Walk silenced her with a shake of his head. He had to think this out. They were too far ahead of him; somebody had planned every move, and whatever he might say now would be turned against him. He was charged with murder. Even in Gainesville they would hang a man for murder. He needed more time to think.

CHAPTER 16

FOR A TIME THAT SEEMED LONG, THERE WAS NO SOUND except the repeated two-syllabled cry of a lone curlew as it swooped up the draw. Its cry ceased abruptly when it dropped to the ground alongside the water.

Then Robinson spoke with obvious loathing. "I don't suppose it's any more crime to kill a one-legged man than anybody else, Freeman, but you can bet your sweet life that my men won't have any compunction if you try to escape."

Walk said stubbornly: "You haven't proved I've done anything yet. You're not a court, Robinson. If I get killed on the way back to Gainesville, there's a lot of people heard you make that threat, Robinson."

The lieutenant looked momentarily uncomfortable.

"You can't bring law to a lawless country by taking it in your own hands," Walk said.

"As far as I'm concerned," Robinson said finally, "I'll deliver you to the court; but there may be others want to take a hand when I'm not looking, Freeman."

"I'll tell you this, Robinson: I'm a hard man to kill; the Apaches had me for twenty-one months, and gave it up." He went on. "If your men do try to murder me and don't put it over, I'm going back to Gainesville and tell the whole story. You've talked too loud, Robinson. You don't dare let me be killed now." Walk was arguing for his life. "Some people might feel called on to tell the truth when they testify under oath. Do you think Miss Hamilton is a perjurer?"

Robinson's face turned a dull red. "All right, Freeman. I'll do my best to get you back alive. But don't take advantage of that promise," he warned.

Walk looked at Ramón. The half-breed was staring intently across the prairie to the southeast.

"Watkins, see that that keg of whisky gets delivered to our camp—and I don't want any samples taken out of it. That's evidence. It has to be delivered in court as is."

Madeline Hamilton spoke up unexpectedly. "Of course," she said, "there is no evidence of illegal sale."

Robinson looked at her with some annoyance. "You people out here on the Plains seem uncommonly well informed on the law," he observed.

"That's not to be unexpected. We've been making our own law, and we've tried to make it right. Of course the keg is circumstantial evidence of murder. And there is the charge of slavery." She paused. "Also, I think you might charge him with accessory after the fact of horse theft."

Walk listened to her recital of the charges, but she was not looking at him. "Ramón has a charge of slavery to answer also."

For an instant Ramón, caught unaware, showed his teeth. "She was not my slave," he said. "She did not belong to me."

Madeline asked quickly, "Whose slave was she?"

Ramón stared at her. He had been fooled momentarily, but not, Walk saw, far enough to reveal the name that Walk would have liked to hear. Ramón lapsed back into his simulation of feeblemindedness. "*No, señorita, no sabe.*"

An expression of contempt and of disappointment went across her face. It was fleeting, but Walk got the startled impression that Madeline Hamilton also was interested in the name of the man behind Ramón.

Robinson did not notice that, and he did not seem

much concerned over Ramón's guilt, but he nodded. "We'll take you for trial, then."

Ramón grinned, nodding, and said, *"Muchísimas gracias, capitán."*

"You'll need to take the mule skinner and Diego and the Indian girl back with you too, won't you?" Madeline asked.

Robinson frowned. Obviously he did not like her tellin' him what to do. "Well—yes, I suppose so."

"After all," said Madeline, "the only way to really clean up things on the Plains is to get to the bottom of the comanchero trade—and this is a wonderful opportunity, it seems to me."

Walk stared at her for an instant. She wanted to uncover the real leader. That much was plain.

Robinson was plainly annoyed, but he took it with good grace. "I'll take everybody on the Plains back if it'll help any, ma'am." He turned to Ramón. "You're under arrest," he said, "charged with slavery."

"Sí, señor," Ramón said, bowing.

"We'll start back in the morning for Fort Griffin," Robinson decided. "There's not much game up here on the Plains, and our supplies won't hold out very long without fresh meat. It looks as if the mud holes are drying up fast too. I'll have Watkins take care of your blue roan, ma'am."

"Thank you."

Walk spoke up. "Miss Hamilton," he said, "in case I don't get to Fort Griffin, I'd like you to have my California sorrel. I think you and she'd understand each other, ma'am."

She looked directly at Walk, her eyes wide—too wide, as though she were covering up. "I don't quite know what to—"

170

"It isn't necessary to say anything, ma'am. Just take good care of her," he said softly. "She's sensitive, ma'am, and she'll appreciate a little affection now and then."

"You better be mighty sure you own that mare before you give her away, Freeman," said Robinson.

Walk did not look at Robinson. "I own her, ma'am," he said to Madeline. "Be gentle with her, will you? Her name is Dulce. She was raised by the Mojave Indians, and remember, she's Indian-broke. That's about the only way you can spook her, ma'am, by mounting on the wrong side. She's pretty touchy about that."

She nodded. Her russet eyes were strangely soft, and she looked away hurriedly.

"Take these three men back to camp, Watkins, and take the Indian girl too. Better tie Freeman's hands for safety. Keep track of that Diego Mexican too. He might be a handy witness."

They walked to camp. It was dark. Watkins tied Walk's hands firmly behind him with a strip of rawhide. He built a small square fence with four picket stakes and a piece of hempen rope. Walk, Estacado, and Ramón were put inside, and, on both east and west, a blue-coated soldier walked back and forth about fifty feet away, the yellow firelight flickering from his brass buttons. Quita had gone with Madeline.

Walk and Estacado sat at one corner against a picket stake, facing Ramón across the square. Walk had chosen the side away from the Army campfires.

"I could untie you mighty easy," Estacado said in a low voice.

Walk said: "That's what Robinson wants—an excuse. He doesn't want to drag five people back to Gainesville for trial."

171

"What if some lowdown maggot-eatin' buzzard tries to knife you in the night?"

"He won't," Walk said, looking hard at Ramón through the darkness. "There'll be one of us awake all the time."

Ramón dropped his pretense of ignorant peasantry. "You worry, eh, *amigo*?"

"I don't believe in it," Walk said. "But if we ever get back to Gainesville, *you're* going to have something to worry about."

Ramón laughed shortly. "They will not put Ramón on trial," he said.

Walk went cold. "You sound mighty confident."

"I am *seguro*," Ramón agreed. "I will not go on trial."

Robinson strode up from the direction of the fires. "Where's your sidekick?" he asked Ramón.

The half-breed shrugged his shoulders helplessly. "*Yo no sé, capitán.*"

Robinson turned on Walk. "Maybe *you* sent him for help. His grullo horse is gone, and there's no chance to find him in the dark. Let's see your hands!" he demanded.

Walk got to his feet. He turned his back to Robinson, who examined his hands thoroughly. "O.K. I just wanted to be sure. It won't go easy with you if I come down here and find you untied, Freeman."

Walk didn't answer.

They were fed with frijoles and heavy, thick-crusted bread. Walk's hands were untied so he could eat.

"Quita's prairie-dog soup is better than this stuff," he said as they retied his hands.

Diego did not show up. Around ten o'clock the soldiers turned in. The fires died down to softly glowing coals.

"Sleep for a couple of hours," Walk told Estacado. "I'll wake you up after a while."

Estacado rolled up in his blankets, buried his head in his shapeless old hat, and was soon snoring. A few minutes later Ramón chucked sardonically through the darkness. "You are not sleepy, my friend."

"Not while you're awake."

"Your hands are tied—no?"

"Don't count on it," Walk warned. "Stay on your own side if you want to be alive for breakfast."

Ramón settled down. Walk could see the half-breed's outline against the red coals of the cook's fire. Those would die down pretty soon, but the moon would be up by midnight. Walk would have gone to sleep anyway, and depended on his alert senses to protect him—but for Diego. The Mexican was out there somewhere, and the confusion of watching in two directions at once might well be fatal. He remained sitting up, and kept his eyes open.

It was very dark. He could not see even the low red cliff down at the comanchero encampment. Over to his left was the picket line. He heard a horse stamping, and presently the sorrel blew the dust out of her nostrils. A coyote barked shortly somewhere in the west; a steer bawled far away, and he wondered why. The cavalry horses began to settle down for the night. One of Walk's mules squealed as another bit him, and there was the solid thud of hoofs on flesh for a moment. Then the swearing of the stable sergeant, and, a moment later, quiet, broken only by the soft, measured tread of the two prisoners' guards, one to the east and one to the west. For a while the night gave out no other sounds. There was only the immensity of the prairie, a huge black bowl with the camp at the bottom of it.

173

The moon came up over the red cliff like an orange disk. That meant dust high in the air, Walk knew, and he wondered, because the wind had died down to a gentle breeze that carried nothing more substantial than the sour, musty odor of the picket line and the strong smell of horse.

He watched the North Star. Around midnight the moon was full, and lit up the sleeping camp, making it like day in reverse. He could see the horses, some standing, some lying. He could make out the white mane and tail of Dulce. The Army wagons stood tall and still, and down at the comanchero encampment the white canvas of the traders' wagons stood out in the moonlight.

He did not call Estacado immediately, for he liked this kind of night; it was peaceful and relaxing, and something from the bigness and the quietness of it seemed to flow into a man's veins and make him a better man for having seen it.

He heard soft footsteps and twisted around quickly. There was an exchange of low voices. Then Madeline Hamilton approached him, followed by the guard. Walk got to his feet. She put out a hand to help him.

"Thank you, ma'am," he said.

"I'm sorry to see you like this." Her voice was genuinely sympathetic but a little clipped, as though to keep him at a distance.

"I'm not sorry," he said, "if it brought you."

"I'd like to ask you some questions," she said.

He glanced at Ramón, who appeared to be asleep. He asked the guard at Madeline's side, "Can't we go off a little way and talk in private?"

"Stand there in the corner and talk low," the guard said, "and don't try anything. The lady gave me her gun."

Walk shrugged.

"I came up here on the Plains with the cavalry," she said in a low voice, "for two reasons: one was to look for the blue roan; the other was to get to the bottom of this comanchero business. The men in the valley were all busy, and I figured the Army needed somebody familiar with the Plains, so as not to overlook any bets."

He nodded understandingly.

"I have a feeling you aren't guilty of *all* the charges made against you." She looked at him earnestly in the soft light of the Comanche moon. "I watched you pull your stuff over the Caprock that morning, and I would have spoken for you today, but you didn't want me to. Why? Why haven't you offered an explanation of the other charges against you?"

Walk looked down at her. He liked the way her eyes glowed in the moonlight. "Ma'am," he said, keeping his voice down, "things seem to have gotten out of hand in a hurry—but the main thing is that Robinson came up here determined to do a job. I was the only one he found when he came to camp, and so he fastened on me first, and naturally he was pleased when the evidence began to point my way. I could have explained things, but that would only have confused him; he wouldn't have turned me loose—and then he would have known my defense." Walk shook his head. "It looked to me like the smartest thing to do was keep still. I figured I'd rather tell my story in court, since I'm going there anyway. And there's another thing, ma'am: there *is* somebody behind the comancheros, working—" He almost said, "working through Ramón," but he checked himself, for even if Madeline were sincere, which he assumed, she might trust the wrong man, and tell him what Walk thought, thereby further curtailing Walk's already short life expectancy. "—working to make trouble he finished lamely, "and if I keep my mouth shut, maybe he will show his hand by the time we get to Gainesville."

She asked, "Do you have any idea who that man is?"

Her voice tipped him off. "Not really, ma'am, not even an honest suspicion. But you do."

She didn't answer that. "I'm sure it isn't you," she said.

"Thank you, ma'am. You won't be sorry for believing in me."

"I hope you can clear up the other charges as well."

He said, "I don't figure on too much trouble, ma'am—if I get to trial."

She touched his arm for reassurance, and went away. He watched her as far as he could see her in the moonlight, and after a while he sat with his back to the picket stake, soaking up strength from the great reservoir of the Plains. One thing was certain: he had to get back to Gainesville, and he had to take Ramón with him. That meant that no matter what Ramón might try to do to him, he dared not kill the half-breed. He wondered if Ramón had figured that out.

He was speculating about that when he saw, beyond the white tops of the wagons and carts at Mucha Que, a dull flash of light on metal, and a moment later the dark forms of men on horseback. He nudged Estacado. Estacado continued to snore. He elbowed him. Estacado rolled over to the other side and kept on snoring. Walk scratched for a handful of dirt and laboriously got to his feet. He stood over Estacado and dribbled the dirt onto the toe of Estacado's boot. Estacado started up fast, sputtering.

Walk said in a low voice, "There's a bunch of riders

176

coming up the draw."

Estacado got to his feet. "Danged if they ain't," he whispered. "It ain't Injuns, neither. They ain't ridin' like they was scared of being seen."

"It isn't soldiers," said Walk presently. "They aren't riding in formation."

"You reckon it's the comancheros comin' back to rescue Ramón?"

"That don't sound reasonable. This here party is ridin' out in the open. If they were aimin' at something like that, they'd at least come up under cover of the mesquite—and they'd wait till the moon goes down. The air's so clear up here on the Plains, it's almost like daylight."

He remembered the reddish hue of the moon when it had arisen, and that puzzled him still more. He didn't think this small party could raise enough dust at a distance to redden the moon. He could count them now—seven riders.

A sentry on the east called, "Halt!"

The party stopped. There were words Walk couldn't hear. Then the sentry led them to the camp. Ramón had come to his feet. Walk thought the half-breed did not act quite as sure as he had at suppertime.

Presently Robinson, with his campaign hat on, strode down to the prisoner pen, followed by the newcomers on foot leading their horses. A trooper with a lighted lantern came running to catch up with them.

Robinson appeared at the rope, big against the night. "This is our haul, gentlemen. We had another one—an old Mexican—but he got away. I doubt that he played any important part in the trouble that has brewed on the Plains. I think we have the real villains right here."

He took the lantern and held it up so that it shone on

the faces of all three—Walk, Estacado, and Ramón. Walk watched Ramón. The half-breed's eyes, large in the darkness but surrounded by a great deal of white, like glazed china, shot to one man so directly that Walk followed his look, to see a black-haired man with concave face, cynical, down-turning mouth, and a reddish-brown calf-skin vest edged with purple velvet. Walk stiffened. That was the man he had fought in the Yellowhouse canyon, the man Madeline Hamilton had called Gault, and there was something about the singling out of him by Ramón's glance that made Walk tighten up. Gault's cold blue eyes went briefly over Ramón, but without any sign of recognition; then he looked at Walk.

Clay Hamilton, small and slight, with a big, thick mustache cut square at each end, stepped out in front; he pulled his peaked-brim hat down harder on his forehead. "Which one is the leader?" he asked.

The information came from an unexpected source. Gault promptly pointed at Walk and said, "That one."

Walk said coldly, "You mean I'm the one who called your play and found out you were bluffing, down in the canyon."

Gault's sallow face tightened into deeper lines. He pulled his big hat down hard on his head.

Wilbarger, short, dark, close-coupled, stepped forward. He wasn't wearing the floppy leather chaps; there wasn't any brush on the Plains to require them. "That's the gent that come up the valley the other day, all right, but what makes you think he's the head comanchero?" He turned on Gault, and the handle of his bowie knife gleamed in the moonlight.

Gault had an answer ready. "Stands to reason. This Mexican sure isn't. I figger this tall gent is the one—and

178

the feller with the black whiskers is his *segundo.*"

Tompkins, tall, lean, thoughtful, was tossing the flattened Minié ball up and down in his palm. "That's no proof," he said judiciously. "It *could* even be evidence the other way."

Robinson said: "All right, gentlemen. You got me out of bed after midnight to look at the prisoners. I don't know how you knew we had them, or whether you just guessed it, but I've got a long day's ride ahead of me tomorrow, and I'd appreciate it if you'd tell me what it's all about."

Clay Hamilton's jaws tightened. His lips were thin. He said in his solid Missouri twang: "The Kiowas raided my place last night at the head of the canyon. We were all having a meeting down at Wilbarger's, and consequently the upper canyon was not well guarded." He paused, and then added harshly: "My man Shorty was riding a big gray that was head-shy and hard to bridle. Shorty had a lame arm anyway. They got him at the corral—and scalped him. So this morning we decided to come up here and see for ourselves. Look at it our way, Lieutenant. Somebody knew we were having that meeting last night, and tipped off the Kiowas. They took every horse in my corrals, and left a dead man and another with a hoop-iron spike in his brain pan. You know what that means: blood poisoning."

"All right," said Robinson, "but what's that got to do with me? I've got some prisoners here, and I'm taking them back to Gainesville for trial."

"Gainesville is a long ways," Gault said harshly. "If you figger you got the right man, we'll have a trial right here."

Walk went cold. Estacado edged near him and began to fumble at the rawhide that tied Walk's wrists. Walk

179

was watching Ramón, and he saw suddenly that Ramón was scared too. If Gault was Ramón's boss, Ramón didn't trust him.

Robinson said coldly, "What are you talking about?"

Newton spoke in his Louisiana drawl. "We got enough men right here to hold court, Lieutenant. You got a man there that caused the murder of a cowboy and the theft of fifteen head of horses. This is the Panhandle, and out here a man's horse is worth his life; we don't fool around with horse thieves, and we don't like men that trade iron to the Indians for arrowheads. We been waitin' five years for justice without gettin' any, and we figger on passin' some out ourselves. We can try him right here and get it over with and save the State of Texas a lot of money."

Tompkins said thoughtfully: "There's a lot in what he says, Lieutenant. There hasn't been any law out here but what we've made ourselves."

Wilbarger said, "I never was one for doin' these things too quick, but we been takin' an awful beatin' from these comancheros at Mucha Que."

Newton's long mustaches hung down both sides of his mouth and gave him a hungry look in the moonlight. "I got a rope. Let's try him. What are we waitin' on, gents?"

Estacado was working hard at Walk's wrists but getting nowhere. But Robinson stopped them short. "You're waiting on me, gentlemen," he said coldly. "These men are prisoners of the United States Army. There is no established court on the Plains, and there will be no prairie-dog court up here. That is lynch law."

Walk drew his wrists away from Estacado and waited tensely.

Newton said ominously, "If we take him, Lieutenant,

what'll you do then?"

"If you take him," Robinson said in a hard voice, "—which I do not believe you can do—I will charge you with obstruction of justice. If you hang him, I will arrest you for murder."

There was an odd light in Newton's eyes. "I've got a pistol in my hand, Lieutenant, that says we take him."

Walk began to edge backward.

But Robinson wasn't fazed. He said, "I've got a bar on my shoulder that says you would never be that crazy. If any of you men know what that means—" He looked at Tompkins and Hamilton. "If any of you men have been Confederate officers, you better tell that hothead it's unhealthy to pull a pistol on the Army."

Clay Hamilton drew a deep breath. "He's right," he said reluctantly. "These fellows are prisoners. We got here too late."

Newton muttered, "You-all were set on administerin' some tightrope justice when we started."

"It's different now," Clay said quietly.

"We rode for twenty-four hours straight," Newton said stubbornly.

"It's no farther back," Clay pointed out. He turned to Robinson. "He's your prisoner, but do you mind if we ride back with you? There might be such a thing as they'd escape."

"You may ride back with me," Robinson said, "but don't count on anything like that."

They left slowly, with backward glances. When they got out of hearing, Estacado whispered jubilantly: "I could kiss him. He never budged an inch."

Walk took a deep breath. "This is the sweetest air I ever tasted," he said, and called in a low voice to Ramón, "What do you think now, *hombre?* Your boss would as soon hang you as me."

Ramón gave away nothing, although he turned slowly. When he was fully around, he was in command of his feelings, and his white teeth glowed in the moonlight. "I theenk," he said slowly, "when so many people want to keel a man, it's a very long road to Gainesville."

CHAPTER 17

IT WASN'T COMFORTABLE SLEEPING WITH TIED HANDS, but Walk managed. He lay on his right side, and when he was awakened by the braying of a wild donkey out on the prairie, his right arm was numb from the shoulder down.

"I could just as well have untied you," Estacado muttered.

"There's too many people around here looking for an excuse to pump me full of lead," Walk said. "I'm walkin' a mighty slippery path, and there's rattlesnakes on both sides."

He stood up and yawned. The air on the high Plains was thinner than it was down below, and the sun, still below the horizon, did not light up a tiny strip along the edge of the sky as it did down at San Antone; instead, the whole eastern half of the sky seemed to come daylight all at once. This hour, too, had an invigorating quality, for there was a very light dew that seemed to give a freshness to the new day. There was not the immediate blast of heat from the sun to take away a man's breath, as it did on the desert; instead, the morning warmed gently, and gave a man time to get used to it and to absorb energy from the sweetened air.

There was a faint fragrance of burning wood. The Army cook had a fire going under a field stove, and the buffalo chips made only a thin wisp of blue smoke that was soon lost in the air. The wind began coming up from the west. The soldiers were down on the picket line, saddling up, talking first gently to their horses, then more loudly, and finally with vehemence punctuated with vigorous profanity.

Walk heard the sorrel whinny. A soldier came with plates of beans and bacon and slabs of cornbread. Robinson was with him. He examined Walk's tied hands, and nodded. "You can ride your sorrel back," he said, "but I'm not taking any chance on your getting away. Your rancher friends would like an excuse to throw lead at you, but my job is to get you before a judge. You can ride with your hands tied and the mare loose, or you can ride with your hands loose and the mare hobbled. What do you say?"

Walk said, "It would kill the mare to crowhop all day long with me on her back."

"And it may kill you if she spooks," said Robinson. "If she throws you, you may land on your head."

"I'll take my chances," Walk said stiffly.

Robinson nodded, as if his respect for Walk had gone up. "I'm turning your cattle over to the ranchmen who showed up last night. They'll push them back with us and take care of them. If they turn out to be yours, you'll get paid for them."

Walk nodded.

"Don't get any wrong ideas over what happened last night," Robinson warned. "I didn't back down those ranchmen for any love of your hide. I still think you're the man we want, and that's the only reason I interfered. Personally, I'd as soon see you hanging from the end of a wagon tongue."

"Your good wishes," Walk said dryly, "are exceeded only by your thoughtfulness for my comfort."

Robinson glared at him. Then he said to Estacado: "Hitch up your mules and get ready to roll. We are leaving in forty-five minutes." He pointed across the draw. "A soldier is taking the mules to your wagon."

Estacado nodded truculently.

Robinson told them all: "We're going to push. We want to hit the Yellowhouse canyon by tomorrow night. We'll water up there and cut south and southeast, the way we came. There's a lake about thirty miles south of the canyon, and we should be off the Plains in a couple of days."

The sorrel was brought up for Walk; he got into the saddle, and a soldier tied his hands behind him. Ramón was given the mustang that had been in Walk's small herd. Madeline Hamilton came out riding the bluc roan, and Quita was bchind her on the rangy bay. Quita's blanket, and Walk's and Estacado's and Ramón's bedrolls were thrown into Walk's wagon.

The sun was barely up when the top sergeant started them out in a column of two's. Clay Hamilton and Madeline rode up in front with Robinson. The soldiers were next. Walk's herd was in behind the troopers, pushed hard by the six ranchmen from the Yellowhouse. Walk and Ramón rode in the thick dust back of the herd, watched always by a soldier guard and one or more of the ranchmen. Quita rode behind Walk, and the wagons came last.

That was a long day in the heat and the dust. They camped at Yellow Lake about sundown, and Walk was glad to be on his feet again. They untied him. He took the saddle off the sorrel and rubbed her down with his hands.

He ate supper with Estacado, and Ramón sat a little way off from them. Sitting back on his heels, Walk felt a sudden urge to look up, and raised his head, to find Ramón's swarthy face turned his way, the black eyes calculating. Walk stared at him. Ramón turned back to his food.

Estacado nudged Walk. "He'll try tonight," he growled.

Walk nodded slowly. "I'll be ready."

"What'll it be with? They took his knife."

"It's easy enough for his boss to slip him one."

They were taken back to the wagon. "I'll sleep under the back end," Estacado said. "You sleep with your head under the front axle. It won't be easy for him to get to you there."

Walk's hands were tied again. His wrists were sore, and the rawhide thongs seemed to cut deeper. Estacado spread a blanket for him on the grama grass, and Walk lay down. The front wheels and the axle and the tongue and doubletree gave some protection.

The camp was settling down. Ramón was not in sight. Estacado said: "I'll stay awake till midnight. You git some sleep."

The sky was dark, but the stars twinkled like brilliant yellow, red, and blue pinpoints from a black bed. "Whatever comes, will come around midnight," Walk answered, "because the moon will be up at one o'clock. I'll be awake until then. You might as well start snoring." He added, "Maybe that'll scare him off."

Estacado grunted uneasily, but he rolled up in his blanket. There were heavy steps in crunching grass, and the lieutenant's voice: "Freeman?"

Walk started to sit up but bumped his head on the

forehound. "Yes?"

"We're out in the middle of nowhere, and I'm going to untie you," Robinson said. "You can't go very far up here on foot—and the horses, including your sorrel, are closely guarded."

Walk came out sitting up, using his spurs to dig into the ground and pull himself forward a few inches at a time. The lieutenant untied him. "Take my advice and don't leave your wagon. My men will shoot if you start roaming around."

"They won't get an excuse to shoot at me," Walk assured him, and rolled under the wagon. He sat with his back against the running gear and rubbed his wrists. It was good to have his hands loose. Presently Estacado began to snore. The sorrel whinnied and settled down for the night. The fires were out. A coyote, far off, smelled the encampment and howled querulously. A guard with a rifle on his shoulder took up a station a hundred yards west of the wagon and began to stride back and forth. Walk lay down for a while, but, when the guard changed at midnight, he sat up quietly. His hat was on the ground near Estacado.

He was almost asleep when he heard a light footstep in the grass. He was instantly awake, and drew back against the running gear and froze.

He watched through the wheel. Against the stars he could see the dark shapes of horses, beginning to lie down. Then something cut off his view of the horses. It also was black against the stars, but it seemed big, and he knew it was close. It moved a little, noiselessly. He watched it through the spokes. It moved to the open space between the front and rear wheels and stooped. The bulk of the man and his round shoulders were enough to identify Ramón. He braced himself with his left hand on the wagon box, and Walk saw the outline of his head. He wasn't wearing the big hat.

The half-breed's right arm came under the wagon while Ramón tried to make out his target. Walk didn't move until the man was off balance. Then he seized the groping right arm with his left, and at the same time threw his right leg behind Ramón's heels and tried to push the man over backward.

But Ramón was like a cat on his feet. He made no outcry, but the breath whistled in through his mouth.

Walk was on his knees, but Ramón jerked his right arm loose. He stabbed Walk, the knife blade slicing through the meat on the bony top of his shoulder. He strained against the man and tried to vault to his feet. But he didn't clear the wagon box. His head crashed against a wooden crosspiece, and for a moment he was dazed, and sank back. Ramón braced his left hand on the wagon box and stabbed at him again.

There was a thud. Ramón gasped, and did not move for an instant. Walk got his senses back. He plunged out from under the wagon and whirled to meet Ramón. The man twisted to meet him, but he did not move freely.

The guard was running toward them in the dark. Walk crashed two blows against Ramón's jaw. Ramón didn't fight back. He tried to evade the attack. Then Walk saw that his hand was pinned to the wagon with a long knife. Walk gripped the knife with both hands and jerked it loose.

Ramón seemed to drop. Walk started after him with the knife, but Ramón scuttled under the wagon and went through.

The guard reached the spot. "What's doing here?" he demanded.

Walk let himself roll down quietly on his back. He

tried to make his voice sound sleepy. "Reckon I was having a nightmare, Sergeant."

The guard said, "Hmph!" hesitated, and then went back. Walk quietly wiped the knife blade on the grass and laid it up on the perch, the long pole that ran under the wagon lengthwise. He thought Ramón would be busy taking care of his hand for a while. His own cut wasn't bleeding much. He wrapped his bandanna around it and went to sleep.

At breakfast Estacado nudged him. "The greaser's got his left hand wrapped up. What's he been up to?"

Walk smiled grimly. "The grasshoppers grow big up here on the Plains," he said. "And they bite hard." He put down his tin plate and walked around to the far side of the wagon. He saw the deep cut made by the point of a knife, and the bloodstain around it. He looked for Quita. She was finishing her breakfast, standing alone. Walk held out his arm with the knife concealed lengthwise beneath it. "You dropped something last night, *señorita,*" he said softly, "at exactly the right time and place. *Muchas gracias.*"

She looked up at him, her eyes big. Then she smiled. She took the knife quietly, and it disappeared inside her clothes. "Is very fast—a knife," she said.

"Hey, Freeman!" That was Robinson's strident voice.

Walk met him on the other side of the wagon. Robinson had the rawhide. "I understand there was some monkey business around your wagon last night. I'm not taking any chances on you, Freeman. You're a valuable man."

Walk turned around. "Tie me up, then. I sure wouldn't want you to lose anything valuable."

That day the sun was hotter and the dust rose thicker. The heat began to sap their strength, and by the time they stopped for dinner, tempers were getting short.

Walk was still able to keep his seat in the saddle, but, without the balancing weight of his arms, he was getting tired. It was a dry stop to eat; the horses were given a handful of corn in a *morral*, or nose bag; the men got beans and biscuits and bacon and short drinks of water. They started out in the heat of the day, with the sun directly overhead and beating down hard with an intensity that would drain a man's tissues of moisture and make his ribs stick through his skin in a few hours.

Madeline started slowly, and presently she was riding alongside Walk's wagon, watching him with some concern. His muscles were getting numb, failing to respond to the movements of the sorrel. He watched Madeline out of the corner of his eye, and presently she spurred forward and was lost to sight. For a while there was nothing but the bawling of thirsty cattle, an occasional snorting to clear dust-laden nostrils, the smell of sweating horses, the creak of prairie wagons, and the stifling dust that settled in thick layers in his dry throat.

He tried to work his bandanna over his nose to keep out the dirt, but he couldn't make it. He had to use his hands on the cantle behind him to hold his balance in the saddle. Then Quita was alongside. She silently opened a canteen and held it to his lips. He managed to get a drink. She used a corner of his bandanna to wipe the dust from his lips, and then lifted the handkerchief so it hung over his nose.

He looked at her and tried to smile. "*Gracias, señorita.*"

Her black eyes were soft as she answered, "*No hay nada, señor.*"

He noticed a cessation of movement ahead and to the

right. Madeline Hamilton and Lieutenant Robinson were sitting their horses watching him. He saw contempt on Madeline's face. Robinson spoke to her. She shook her head and wheeled the blue roan angrily back toward the front of the column. Walk took a deep breath and put his attention on staying in the saddle.

Past the middle of the afternoon, they stopped for a breather. Walk, with the help of his guard, dismounted and walked forward to get out of the dust, with Estacado at his side.

Madeline was talking to Robinson. "It's less than ten miles," she said, "and I know the country perfectly."

Robinson nodded. "Be careful," he urged. "It's Comanche country, you know."

"I know," she said. She rode back to where her father was sitting on the ground with Gault, the thoughtful Tompkins, long-mustached Newton with his powder horn, the short, close-coupled Wilbarger with his bowie knife, and the others.

"Mighty good time they're makin' with that herd," Estacado noted.

Walk agreed. "I doubt I'll have much left when we reach the Yellowhouse, though. That bunch of steers is beginning to look wall-eyed."

"They're tough critters," Estacado pointed out. "They ain't used to getting water regular."

Madeline spoke to her father, then wheeled the blue roan and rode away at a lope, pointedly ignoring Walk. He wondered where she was going and why.

He went up to the ranchmen and spoke to Clay Hamilton. "What do you aim to do with my stock?" he asked.

Clay Hamilton looked up at him and slowly got to his feet. Wilbarger fingered the handle of his bowie knife.

Dow Jones was leaning back on his arms with his bad leg stretched out in the heavy sheepskin chaps. Newton's eyes brightened with the unhealthy gleam of temper, and Tompkins quit tossing the Minié ball up and down in his hand.

Clay Hamilton pulled his curled hatbrim tighter and said, "Why are you askin'?"

"Because I want to know."

Wilbarger said, "They ain't yours anyway."

"They're mine," Walk said positively, "until somebody proves otherwise, and I demand the same consideration you would expect from me."

"You ain't giving us any consideration," Newton said quickly.

"That's a question for the courts," Walk reminded him. "I've asked for consideration from you," he told Clay Hamilton. "I'm a comanchero for the present, and I'm not apologizing for it. I got in with a bad bunch, maybe, but I didn't come to steal your stuff. And remember this: I don't care what it looks like now; I'm not guilty of any of these charges, and I'll prove it in court. I'm coming back. I'm going to have a ranch up here on the Plains. I'd rather figger I can deal with you on the square."

Gault stood up, and powerfully now Walk sensed his bigness and his dangerousness. Gault said: "You're a prisoner. You've got no right to ask anything. We'll wait till you get back—if you *get* back."

"I'm a prisoner but not yet a criminal—and even a criminal has rights," Walk reminded them.

Clay Hamilton took a deep breath and said in his Missouri twang: "I'll see you get justice on the stock. The bronc isn't branded, and he's probably yours. The steers are branded, but they're new brands and we don't know them. If I decide they belong to you, I'll take care of them, and you'll get them back less a reasonable charge for their keep, or the difference in money, when you come back. And I might as well say with Gault—*if* you come back."

Robinson was coming toward them at a lope. Walk turned away. Estacado helped him up on the sorrel. Estacado said, "You could get killed makin' a play like that."

Walk grinned as Estacado adjusted the bandanna over his nose. "Not so much as it looks," he said. "In fact, I was takin' advantage of them. There are only two men there who would shoot a man with his hands tied behind his back—Newton and Gault—and the others wouldn't let them."

"What good did it do you to show off, then?"

"It did a lot of good," said Walk. "It served notice on them that I still consider those cattle my property, and it put Clay Hamilton on his honor to take care of them; also, I've made them think I'm not scared of them, and they may go slow on rough stuff."

"You *are* scared, aren't you?" Estacado asked curiously.

Walk fastened his gray eyes on the old man. "Did you ever try walkin' the top wire of a fence through a field of prickly-pear cactus four feet deep?"

Estacado shuddered. "Do I look like my rear end is made out of buffalo neck-hide?"

Walk said soberly, "I reckon walkin' a wire is better than walkin' on air."

"Just the same," said Estacado, "you're the dernedest gent I ever seen to serve notice when you got nothin' to back it up with." He stared at Walk a moment. "And I'll be hornswoggled if some way or other you didn't make

192

Christians out of 'em, too. I don't see how you do it."

"Because I mean it," said Walk.

"In your boots," Estacado said, "it ain't in the picture. You'll be lucky to get off the Plains alive."

"There's nothing impossible," Walk said philosophically, "but what you think is impossible. Some things are unlikely, I'll grant, but not impossible—and Clay Hamilton knows that."

The command, "Prepare to mount!" rang out at the front of the train, and Estacado went to his wagon. The dust again rose thick and stifling, and Walk's muscles began to rebel at the task of holding him upright. Then he saw the reddish-brown-vested Gault riding on the left, out of the dust, and watching the horizon on the north and northeast. Walk edged over that way, guiding the sorrel with his knees. He watched the horizon but saw nothing.

Another hour went by. Quita came silently from behind with a canteen. Walk drank lightly and said, *"Gracias, señorita."*

"Que besa sus pies," she said humbly. "I am your servant."

He smiled, and wondered how she would take it when the Army sent her back home. Pretty hard, maybe; she didn't want to go home. He'd miss her too—but he didn't know what else to do with her.

The sun was starting down in the west, but it was still hot, and the stiff dry wind that came from the west bore heat that shriveled men and animals. Again Walk moved out to the left, and again he saw Gault watching the horizon, but again Walk saw nothing.

But a moment later a shout went up. A small cloud of dust was coming rapidly from the northeast. Somebody was fogging it toward the cavalry train.

193

Walk pushed the sorrel forward in time to see Madeline Hamilton pull up on the blue roan. The horse was dark with sweat, and on his chest and flanks and around the saddle blanket he was caked with salt.

Madeline pulled him back on his haunches before Lieutenant Robinson. "Kiowas!" she cried. "Hundreds of them! They're waiting below the Caprock!"

Robinson asked sharply, "How'd you find out?"

Her russet eyes were large. "I started down the trail into the Yellowhouse and ran straight into them. They came boiling out of the canyon in full paint and war bonnets and howling murder." She shuddered and rubbed the blue roan's sweating withers. "They chased me, but the roan outran them."

"Where are they now?"

"They gave up and seemed to stop to talk it over. They didn't chase me any more."

Walk looked again at the horizon. He knew now why the moon had been red two nights before. But why had Gault been watching the northeast?

CHAPTER 18

ROBINSON ASKED SERIOUSLY, "YOU THINK THE Indians are on the warpath, ma'am?"

Clay Hamilton rode up. His horse was limping on the right front foot. "If they're waiting below the Caprock," he said sharply, "they're waiting for *us*."

"I thought the Plains Indians didn't fight in full dress."

"They don't. It sounds to me as if Madeline surprised them before they were ready."

"You say hundreds of them?" Robinson asked

194

Madeline.

"It was a big war party," she said. "I'm sure there were well over a hundred who came out of the canyon. They seemed to be coming over the Caprock as long as I could see."

"They didn't follow you very far. It looks like an ambush to me. We'll turn southeast and go around them. You folks," he said to Hamilton, "will be able to find a way down the Caprock for us, won't you?"

"There are old comanchero trails," Clay Hamilton said. "We'll manage."

Tompkins said thoughtfully, "The Kiowas and Comanches don't generally fool around. Now that they're discovered, they should be coming on to attack."

"My scouts have been southeast," Robinson said, "and haven't seen any sign of Indians there. It doesn't look like a trap."

Clay Hamilton shook his head. "It sure doesn't sound like them to hang back, but if we turn southeast we'll be able to keep in the open, at least. There won't be any water, and we'll have to make a dry camp tonight; but we can travel late, and if you throw out your scouts behind we'll have time to get ready for them when they come."

"An hour or so more and it'll be dark," said Robinson. "Will they attack in the dark?"

"Not as a rule," said Hamilton. "But you can't bet your life on it."

The train turned southeast. It was still hot and the dust was thick, and the wind, blowing strongly and with unceasing pressure from the west, seemed to come from the heart of a furnace. There was the added knowledge on the part of the men that there would be a dry camp. The animals seemed to sense it too, and some of them,

195

especially the mules, did not want to turn from their course. Robinson sent a scout and a party to guard along the left flank, while the point operated far ahead and wide-spread. There were some sixty troopers all told, besides seven ranchers, Walk and Estacado, Ramón, and the two women. All armed, they would make a formidable force, but they would not be too many in event of a full-scale attack.

Clay Hamilton and Madeline rode on the left of the column at the rear of the small herd of cattle. The wind from the west was carrying most of the dirt away from the diagonal course of the train, but the left side was the danger side, and presently Robinson joined them. Walk heard Clay ask Madeline, "Did you see Quanah Parker?"

"I don't think Quanah's people were there," she said. "There were Comanches with them, and maybe Cheyennes, but I don't know what clans—and I'm sure the raid was in charge of Kiowas."

"With all three tribes represented," Clay said, "it sounds like a serious effort to wipe out this party and drive the white man off the Plains for good. What I don't understand is: how did they know where and when to expect us? The scouts haven't reported any signs of Indians, and there were none when we came through day before yesterday."

"An Indian can go where a white man can't see him," Wilbarger observed.

"True enough for one Indian, but lone Indians don't generally get too far from the tribe; when there's a bunch like this around it's easy to keep an eye on them. No," he said doggedly, "this bunch came here to ambush us. They must have had information in advance as to where we were headed and when we would get there, and then they gathered their tribes to the northeast of the Caprock where they would not be observed, and sometime today they slipped into the canyon below the Caprock to wait for us. They sure didn't figure on staying there all night just on speculation. Indians don't work that way." He got down from the saddle, pulled his horse's right front leg off the ground, and examined the frog. He found nothing, and put it down.

"They figured on getting up against the Caprock and then circling," Robinson suggested.

"Worse than that," said Tompkins. "They would have waited until about half of us got down into the canyon. The soldiers would have taken the stock down the trail to water. Then the Indians would have had us all split up. It would have been a massacre."

"It may be yet," Hamilton said soberly. "Madeline must have ridden into them before they were ready, or she'd never have seen a one. They can hide in this country like a horny toad. And that's another argument that they knew exactly when to expect us." He pulled his hatbrim tighter. "It was a lucky break for us that Madeline surprised them."

"I still don't understand," said Tompkins, "why they didn't follow her to attack immediately." He looked apprehensively to the south. "You don't reckon they're fooling us some way on that side too?"

Robinson said, "My scouts are positive that if there are any Indians within reach in that direction there are not more than a handful."

Clay said dubiously, "I don't know how a handful could hurt us, but they sound mighty sure of themselves."

The train moved steadily until just before complete darkness. Walk was very tired. The mules began to balk, and Robinson stopped the train. He told Estacado: "Follow my wagons and pull into a circle. We'll have to put the horses in the center."

The three wagons began to pull together. The troopers prepared to lead their horses in for protection. Quita rode to the rear end of Walk's wagon, dismounted, and let down the tailgate to get the bedrolls.

But there were thundering hoofs on the prairie. Walk looked to the right. The three soldiers who had been on point were galloping back to the train, and a distant, terrifying cry rolled over the Plains:

"Prairie fire!"

Walk stared. Beyond them, where a moment before there had been only blackness in the south, there was a leaping wall of red-and-yellow fire.

Robinson pounded back to Clay Hamilton and Tompkins. "What's your idea on this?" he shouted.

"The Indians set it," Clay said promptly. "See how it sprung up on a wide front?" He watched it from under the pointed brim of his hat. "That's why they didn't follow Madeline back today. They were planning this all the time. There's a stiff west wind, and the fire is traveling fast. I doubt we could outrun it to the east, and it's too far behind us to try to go around to the west. We better stop where we are, I'd say, and start a backfire— but don't make camp. When the Indians come, we may have to move."

"Do you think the Indians will attack us now?"

"Absolutely," said Clay.

"It doesn't sound good."

"It sure doesn't."

Robinson said, "I'll throw out guards to the north and west. Will you take charge of the fire fighting?"

Clay nodded briefly. "How many men can you

198

spare?"

"Twenty-five."

"Send them back here." He turned to Tompkins. "Kill a steer," he said, and Tompkins pulled his .36 Colt and walked into the little herd. He aimed the muzzle just under a steer's ear and pulled the trigger. The steer's knees began to buckle. It went down in a heap.

Clay snapped at Wilbarger. "Cut off its head."

The soldiers came back at a lope. Clay got them together and said: "Get all the gunny sacks you can find. Fill them half full of dirt, and tie a rope to the neck of each sack. Get back here in not more than ten minutes. Two of you get axes." The soldiers scattered.

Clay said to Wilbarger. "Split it down the belly."

Wilbarger's hands were already bloody. With Newton's help he rolled the carcass on its back and went to work with his long-bladed bowie knife. The two soldiers came back with axes. Clay took one axe and cut the ribs on one side along the backbone. MacLeod cut the others. The carcass began to flatten out.

"Now turn it over," Clay said, "and a couple of you get in there and crush up the bones."

The soldiers began to lope back with filled gunny sacks. By that time the carcass was a mass of wet flesh.

The south and west was a racing wall of fire. The smell of burning grass was strong, and bits of ash began to drift down on the men. The fire extended along a straight line parallel with their course, about a mile away, and from about two miles behind them to about a half mile east of their position. Under the drive of the wind it was advancing east on a broad diagonal front. If it burned on without a change, it would gradually come over their position; if the wind should swing into the southwest it would advance on them very rapidly.

Wilbarger and MacLeod mounted. Wilbarger's lariat was tied to a front foot of the steer's carcass; MacLeod's was tied to a hind foot.

Dow Jones had a tight bundle of brush. He tied one end of his rope around the bundle and lit it with a match, then trotted his horse along a line parallel with the fire but only about three hundred yards from their camp site. The thick, dry grass caught like tinder as the fagot was trailed. Wilbarger and Newton waited a moment until the grass began to burn; then, one on each side of the burning strip, they dragged the wet carcass over the edge of the burning strip nearest the camp, while they let the other side burn toward the main fire. Men followed them on foot, spotting the small fires that developed after the drag had passed. Occasionally a burning area, fanned by the wind, got out of control, and there was a shout for the drag. Then Wilbarger and MacLeod would come back at a gallop, dragging the carcass.

The two men on the drag had to change horses before long, but in half an hour the men had burned a strip a hundred yards wide about the camp in a quarter-circle. The grass on the opposite side on the strip was still burning, but slowly, for it was against the wind. The men stayed out there, patrolling the strip for new outbreaks.

By that time the main fire roared fifty feet into a black sky, and at times the clouds of smoke became so dense the fire was hidden for a moment, only to break out in new fury when the clouds parted—and always nearer. The gray clouds rolled toward them on the wind, bearing the stench of burned grass and scorched flesh. An antelope appeared between the two fires and began to run in a circle. A pair of coyotes loped down the alley between the fires, running with their tails forward and howling steadily. Walk's small herd of steers had stood stone-still for half an hour. Now they broke. They turned in unison. They curled their tails and stampeded toward the Caprock.

The sky was dense black. No stars were visible in the glare of the flames. They could hear the crackle of burning grass, and a sound seemed to issue from the ground like the rumble of the cavernous earth under the stampeding hoofs of a tremendous herd. The wind began to carry flaming torches of grass high in the air.

Walk and Estacado stood by their wagon and watched. Estacado said, "The wind better not change on us."

Then above the crackle and rumble of the fire came another cry: "Indians!"

The fire had lighted up the prairie, and a mile to the north Robinson's flanking scouts were kneeling and firing. Gunshots floated back. The scouting party retreated slowly toward camp, then leaped onto their horses and came back at a gallop.

Walk gasped. The plain beyond the scouts was suddenly filled from one side to the other with a mass of advancing Indians. They began to yell as they broke into a charge after the soldiers.

Robinson's strong voice barked orders. Troopers lay down behind saddles and stood behind wagons or lay flat in the grass, bracing their long rifles and beginning to fire quietly and steadily. One of the returning guards dove head-first from his horse with an arrow protruding from his back. The arrow broke as he rolled over on the ground. Then the Indians rode over the body and came on.

Arrows fell in the camp, and Indians began to drop

from their saddles. They turned to the left in a column and swept by, firing broadside, emitting the ululating yell that had curdled the blood of the first man on the Plains. They swept by and went back around in a great circle, firing as they came back in range. Some had guns, and the white canvas of the wagons began to show punctures.

The troopers were concentrated around the wagons, and the horses were tied as much as possible in the protection of the wagons. Madeline Hamilton was firing her six-shooter from the corner of Walk's wagon.

Walk, his eyes on the Indians as they swept past, asked, "Did you ever see an Indian wear a straw hat?"

Estacado stared at the attackers. "Not before now," he said. "There sure is one out there, though."

Walk observed, "There are some war bonnets too. That probably means Cheyennes. It looks like they're pretty set on cleaning us out."

"I don't doubt," said Estacado, "there'll be some hair lifted before this is over."

Robinson had come up behind them. "I think we can hold them off. They haven't too many guns and they don't use them too well. We're taking a toll. They could charge us, but they don't like hot lead in their faces."

Walk, with his hands still tied behind him, said: "They seldom attack head-on. We'll be all right if the wind holds."

Robinson looked at him. "Hamilton has got the backfire under control, hasn't he?"

Walk nodded. "They've done a good job there."

"Then it doesn't matter about the wind."

But Walk looked back at the raging wall of fire under the billowing clouds of smoke. "The wind died down a minute ago," he said.

"All the better."

Walk did not answer. He didn't need to. At that moment a dozen scattered firebrands swirled high over their heads and landed in the dry grass fifty feet to the north of the wagons. Robinson ran out with two men and beat the spots out with blankets while arrows fell around them and the soldiers in camp tried to cover them with rifle fire. The three got back unhurt. Walk was watching the south. Blazing bunches of grass were being whipped into the air by a wind that was stronger than it had been before.

Robinson said incredulously, "It can't change that fast."

Walk looked at the black sky. Clay Hamilton appeared. His face was blistered and his eyebrows singed. His hands were black from the soot of burned grass, and his hat was covered with dead ash. He shouted at Robinson over the din, "We've got to get out. If we stay here we'll be fried!"

Robinson listened for an instant to the crackle and rumble of the fire, the yelling of the Indians, the whistling and zip of arrows into canvas, the thud of black-powder rifles. He saw a man fall with an arrow in his ribs. He took a deep breath of the air that smelled equally of burning grass and powder smoke, and asked, "Where to?"

Clay Hamilton pointed east. "We've got to race the fire. Only chance is to get around it before it reaches the Caprock and cuts us off."

"How far to the Caprock?"

"Two or three miles."

"We can't make it."

"We might. It isn't traveling east as fast as it was."

"All right," said Robinson, "call in your men."

Clay Hamilton rode off toward the backfire. Robinson shouted orders. Walk felt a tug at his wrists. His hands came free. He looked around and saw Quita calmly putting her bowie knife back in her waist. He nodded brief thanks to her. The soldiers were stringing out, racing east. Brands dropped profusely in the open, creating a burning area between them and the Indians, who rode their circuit just beyond the flames and fired at the riders as they went by.

Robinson stayed until all were gone. Clay Hamilton's horse was limping badly. Two soldiers were hurt. One was bleeding freely from the ribs; the other had a bullet in his arm. They both were able to ride. Clay Hamilton's backfiring crew was dirty and grimy and blistered, but unhurt. Estacado whipped his mules down the lane between the fires. The two Army wagons were behind.

Walk, on the sorrel, had no trouble now keeping up with Estacado and the wagon. Madeline and Quita were just ahead of him. The ranchmen were strung out all along the train. Four troopers brought up the rear. The lane ahead narrowed steadily, the fire coming in closer on both sides.

Robinson rode up alongside Walk. He glanced at Walk's freed hands, but he handed him his gun belt and pistol. He shouted at him, "Report to Fort Griffin if you get out alive."

Walk nodded. Robinson dropped the brass-framed Henry rifle in the wagon with Estacado. Then he went to the rear. Ramón was having trouble with the mustang. It had not been fed for such hard work, and was tiring fast. Robinson tossed Ramón his gun belt. "Report to Fort Griffin," he ordered.

For the first time Walk noticed the half-breed. Ramón's eyes were big, the whites unusually prominent, and his black pupils seemed to protrude from his face. His cheeks were ashy-gray and his hands trembled as he stared at the fire. He was ready to crack wide open, Walk thought.

CHAPTER 19

CLAY HAMILTON DROPPED BACK, MADELINE WITH HIM. "Unhitch those horses!" he shouted at Robinson, "and let 'em run for it. The wagons'll never make it. They're holding us back."

They were galloping side by side. "What about that stuff blowing over us?" Robinson asked.

"It isn't blowing as bad as it was, but we can't stop now. We can't backfire on the north because of the Indians."

There were patches of burning grass on their left. The Indians were weaving among the blazes, keeping up their running broadside of arrow fire, but the soldiers and ranchmen were shooting often enough, with the help of the grass fires, to keep the Indians from closing in to effective range. The Army wagons stopped, and the drivers vaulted from their seats to unfasten the traces, while the four troopers in the rear guard took cover behind the wagons to fire at the Indians and keep them at a distance.

Walk reached his spans of mules before Estacado. He seized Agathy's near tug in one hand and tried to force her back to unsnap it from the singletree. Estacado was running for the breast straps, when Gault charged back on his blaze-faced dun and shouted at Madeline, "Come on, let's get out of here!"

Walk glanced up. At first he thought the man had

gone loco. Then he saw Gault was stone-sober.

"We can't beat the fire!" Gault shouted.

Madeline's reddish golden hair was loose about her head; her face was a little gray from the fine ash that had settled on it, and her forehead was smudged where she had brushed her hair away from her eyes. She looked at Gault levelly but immovably. Her voice was clear through the noise of wind and fire, of galloping horses and screeching Indians, of rifle shots and hoarse commands. "I'll stay with the train, Gault," she said firmly.

Gault's chest swelled beneath the calfskin vest. Walk paused to watch. What was eating on Gault? Maybe he *had* dropped a stirrup, and Madeline, who obviously did not want to go with him, might need help. Walk stepped near. Gault was kicking the dun around to face her. "You fool!" he cried. "If we stay here the Indians'll get us too!"

Walk took a step nearer Gault. "If you don't stay with the train," he asked, "how do you figure on getting through the Indians?"

Gault turned a furious face on him. "I'll get through!" he roared.

There was commotion on the other side of Gault. Ramón had come loping up, raking the mustang with his spurs. His high voice said: "You take me with you, boss! You not leave Ramón!"

Gault stared at the slack face and glazed eyes of the half-breed, and Walk saw the rage build up in Gault at Ramón's words.

Ramón was no longer a rational being. Those were the first words he had uttered since the start of the fire, and now he went to pieces like a crazed horse in a burning barn. He pawed Gault. Gault struck him in the face. Ramón's gun was in his gun belt, but he didn't try to use it. He kept pawing at Gault and saying, "You take Ramón too."

Gault struck him again. Ramón reeled in the saddle. Then he fell against Gault, clawing at him. Gault tried to push him off. He hit him in the face, but Ramón clung. The blaze-faced dun, unnerved by the fire and excitement, moved, and they fell off together.

Gault was up first. "*Jumento!*" he roared.

Ramón was on all fours, getting to his feet. "You take me, too, boss." Gault kicked him under the chin with all the strength of his big legs. Ramón's square-topped black hat seemed to explode from his head.

Clay Hamilton and Wilbarger were watching. Wilbarger looked blank. Hamilton had a puzzled frown on his face. Robinson was coming up from the Army wagons. Estacado was still trying to loosen the mules.

Walk stepped up to Gault. He looked him between the eyes. "He called you 'boss,' " he said.

Gault glared at him. A warning flicker came in Gault's pale blue eyes, but Walk, now having an audience that included Madeline, Clay Hamilton, Wilbarger with his bloody hands, the tall, lean Tompkins, and Lieutenant Robinson, pressed his point.

"Ramón was boss at Mucha Que, and *he* called you boss." Walk felt a tingling in his arms as his numbed muscles began coming back to life, and his fingers felt like thick pieces of mesquite root, but this was his chance to clear himself. It wasn't the best place to settle an argument, with the sky reddened by reflections of red flames from roiling gray clouds, with the subterranean rumble of the fire and the yelling of blood-hungry Indians for a background, and with the smell of burning grass in his nostrils, but there might never be another opportunity like this. They were holding him primarily as secret boss of the comancheros, and if he could back down Gault now, the worst of his troubles would be over.

"You were the man behind the comancheros," he said. "You put up the money. You tipped off the Indians where to raid. You took charge of the stolen goods and sold it." He paused for an instant. "You killed buffalo up on the Plains to cut down the food supply so the Indians would be more willing to raid. Gault, *you set the Indians on us!*" He waved an arm at the prairie and the moving, yelling Kiowas and their allies. "You told them where to wait for us."

"You're crazy!" Robinson said, but more in bewilderment than in assurance.

Walk never took his eyes from Gault. "If that isn't so," he asked, *"how come Diego is out there with the Indians in his straw hat?* Diego is your messenger. He's the one who told the Indians where to wait for us. He's out there now, waiting for you to come, so he can tell the Indians not to kill you!"

Gault's face turned white. Walk would never know why he waited so long—perhaps because the charge was so unexpected it stunned him. Then he whipped up his six-shooter.

Walk's .44 was in his hand, but a red-splotched fist chopped down on Gault's forearm and his bullet went into the dirt. Walk held his fire.

Robinson said: "Put your hardware up. Freeman, give me your gun. You provoked him into drawing."

Walk looked hard at him. "You can't disarm me now," he said. "That would be murder." He slid the gun back into his holster.

Robinson looked at him coldly. His own gun

appeared in his hand. "Give me your gun," he said. "You're still a prisoner."

Walk stood firm. The lieutenant would reach for his gun, but Walk did not intend to give it up.

Then a clear, soft voice spoke up behind him. "You must not take his peestol, *señor capitán*. *El señor* Gault weel kill him because Andale has told the truth—*verdad*. *El señor* Gault is the beeg boss of the comancheros."

Clay Hamilton stared at her an instant and then looked at Gault. Walk saw amazement on Hamilton's face and then seriousness as Hamilton wondered if there were truth in the charge. Quita stayed behind Walk. Walk kept his broad back turned to protect her, and watched Gault. Gault's face began to turn dark red.

The pistol drooped hesitantly in Robinson's freckled hand.

Quita went on hurriedly. "Ramón put the keg in Andale's wagon," she said. "Ramón killed *el señor* Pegleg."

Robinson's eyes flared. He barked at her. "Why didn't you tell me this before?"

"Ramón said he would cut my throat. I want' to wait till he is in the *juzgado*—in jail."

Gault spluttered words like hot coals. "She doesn't know what she's saying! She's a damn' ignorant Indian squaw. She'd sell her soul for a pot of frijoles."

There was silence for a second after Gault's words, and then the crackle of gunfire and the yells of the Indians and the rumble of the prairie fire rushed into the empty space. Madeline Hamilton, sitting straight on the big blue roan, slight against the size of the horse, with the flames making a reddish-brown halo around her hair, said clearly above the sounds of the wild night:

"I believe the girl is right. I've suspected Gault for some time. I never liked the way he disappeared up on the Plains so often." She spoke directly to Gault, as his pale blue eyes shifted slowly to meet hers. "I figured you wanted the head of the canyon so you could work closer with the comancheros," she said. "Last summer I asked the Army to send a detachment out here, and when they did come I came with them, to see for myself. When Lieutenant Robinson arrested Walk Freeman, I didn't know what to think. I wanted everybody taken back to court for trial, so everything would be brought out in the open. But you didn't want Walk Freeman to go to trial, Gault. You didn't dare have the story come out. You set the Indians on us to destroy the train, and especially to get rid of Walk Freeman and Ramón. That's why you want to ride out there now to the Indians. You told them you would join them, and they're expecting you. They won't hurt you if you leave the train now!"

Ramón was clinging to the saddle of Gault's dun. His eyes were shut tightly against the glare of the fire. "You take Ramón too, boss."

Gault's calfskin vest swelled like the body of a scared horned toad. He made a running leap toward Madeline, landing in the saddle in front of her and plowing his spurs into the blue roan's ribs. The horse leaped through the ring of men. Wilbarger was knocked over, and the horse went straight toward the moving Indian lines.

Pistols were in a dozen hands, but Gault was covered by Madeline's body. They saw her pistol come out of the holster, but Gault slapped it into the grass. The blue roan steered between two small islands of burning grass.

Walk did not wait. He vaulted onto the sorrel and set out after them. If Gault ever reached the Indian lines, neither he nor Madeline would ever be seen again by white men, for Gault could never come back.

The blue roan was a powerful horse, but the sorrel was faster. Walk thought he could catch them before they crossed the three hundred yards of open grass between the Indians and the train.

Clay Hamilton turned his horse, but Walk was already past him. Wilbarger bounced to his feet. Robinson shouted: "Everybody forward! We've got to outrun the fire!"

The sorrel was strung out. Walk glanced back quickly to see if anybody was following him.

The rear end of the train lurched forward. The soldiers up ahead strung out in a hard gallop; the ranchmen kept up with them. The horses of the Army wagons, all freed but the saddle animals, now being ridden by the drivers of the wagons, ran at full speed, with their traces dragging.

Only Clay Hamilton and Estacado failed to move up with the rest. Hamilton rode out a little way, watching the race toward the Indian lines, and sat his horse, oblivious to the fire behind him and the target he made for the Indians. He was a pathetic figure, sitting his horse undecided, a little hunched up, and helpless because he knew his lame horse could never match the speed of the two ahead, and also aware that if he should by any chance catch up with them he would never get back, for now he didn't have the rifles of the train for protection against the Indians. The train was gone, and his daughter was gone, and there was nothing he could do but trust Walk Freeman and the sorrel—and hope.

All this Walk saw and understood, and then a powder flash almost in his face brought his attention back to the front. Gault was firing at him, but Madeline wrestled

211

Gault for the pistol and forced him to drop it.

The blue roan pounded on, but the sorrel closed in on the left. Walk leaped at Gault. The roan stumbled under the new weight, and Walk and Gault fell off on the right side. Walk bounced to his feet and launched a fist at Gault. The big man took it and came back, hitting hard. Madeline turned the roan and came back to them. Dulce stopped and circled, waiting.

Walk discovered then that he could not hurt Gault with his fists. The calfskin vest was too thick and was probably padded. Walk had to hit the man in the face to hurt him at all. But every time he hit him in the face he took two or three in the stomach, and they were punishing. He reached both hands and seized Gault's vest, ripped it open and tore down. But in that act he was defenseless. Gault's big fists thudded on his chin, and he felt his arms weaken.

Gault saw that, and spun around to the sorrel. He snatched her reins and vaulted into the saddle. But the sorrel hid her head between her front legs and began to pitch fence-cornered. Gault had made the mistake of mounting the Indian-broke horse on the left side—and the mare was a gut-twister when she dug in.

Walk heard a terrific banging behind him, and looked to see Estacado driving the four-mule team furiously across the prairie toward them, yelling and swearing alternately, and digging chunks out of the mule's rumps with his pistol-shot bullwhip. Walk saw the big hogshead of bread rise into the air from the open end gate and land hard on the prairie, rolling over and over, scattering newspaper-wrapped pones. Ramón, bareheaded, was riding the exhausted mustang behind the wagon, beating the horse with the reins.

Then Gault left the saddle of the sorrel in a rainbow

spin. He landed on all fours. The sorrel stopped abruptly and stepped toward Walk. Walk's head was clear now. As Estacado rattled up behind him in the wagon, with the rifle in his hands, Walk ran at Gault. Gault surged to his feet, but Walk hit him in the stomach once, twice, three times. Gault retreated in a circle. Walk followed. Gault brought up against the end gate of the wagon, saw the handle of a grubbing hoe sticking halfway out, and seized it with both hands. He took a cut at Walk that swung him halfway around. Walk looked at the wagon, saw the handle of the other grubbing hoe, and grinned. He picked it out of the wagon and faced Gault. He saw the first surge of terror cross Gault's pale blue eyes, and then the man swung.

Walk pulled back. The heavy, sharp, crosswise blade shaved his stomach and cut a button off of his wildcat-skin vest. He chopped down at Gault, but missed. Gault swung backhanded, but that was a bad swing and he couldn't control it. Walk cut at him, but Gault moved in and took the blow from the wooden handle inside of the blade. He shortened his own hold and chopped down at Walk's head, but Walk crossed his hoe in time to stop it.

He saw Estacado trying to get behind Gault with the rifle, but shook his head. Ramón, glaze-eyed, sat the trembling mustang, and Estacado held the rifle on him.

Gault swung again, but Walk caught the blade with his own. The steel threw sparks, and then Walk backed away, feinting for an opening. But Gault had seen Estacado with the rifle and backed into the wagon between the front and rear wheels to cover his rear. He brought up against the water keg and stopped. Walk cocked the grubbing hoe over his shoulder and stalked him. Gault made a weak swing but was hampered by the wagon. Walk fixed his eyes on Gault's and came in. He

213

had one last sight of Gault's thin brown hair, his white, concave face and cynical mouth, and one brief glimpse of horror in Gault's bulging, pale blue eyes as the wide blade went for his face.

Then Walk dropped the hoe and sprang for the traces of the mules. The Indians were beginning to close in cautiously. Estacado got the breast straps; they dropped the wagon tongue and turned loose three mules. Estacado mounted Agathy and headed back for the train, sending the three loose mules ahead of him toward the Caprock with fireworks from his bullwhip and a rising crescendo of mule talk. Walk threw a glance at Madeline. She was staring at Gault's mutilated body as if hypnotized. He shouted at her: "Get going!"

Ramón was staring dazedly at the body too. At Walk's shout he looked up. He stared at the wall of fire on the west and south, then abruptly wheeled the mustang and headed for the Indians.

Madeline swung the blue roan, and they cut back toward the open lane at an angle. Clay Hamilton met them, with a quick, grateful handshake for Walk. To the west, behind them, the two Army wagons were on fire. The entire area where they had first stopped was now a plain of blazing grass. Walk swept the north with a glance, in time to see Ramón, with arrows bunched in his chest, throw out his arms, fall backward over the cantle, and slide down the mustang's rump to the ground. Without his black hat, and on a strange horse, he had not been recognized by Diego in time to be saved.

Walk, Madeline, and Clay Hamilton galloped east behind Estacado, with Walk watching Hamilton's horse to grab the man if the horse went down.

The Indians were looting Walk's wagon. Then Walk

saw that the soldiers had stopped up ahead. Robinson had flung out a line of foragers to keep the Indians back, and now the troopers lay on their stomachs in the tall grass with rifles ready. Robinson pointed to the wall of flame, which seemed to have stopped entirely its progress toward the east and was advancing slowly but steadily north, closing in on them, while the Indians waited on the northwest.

"We're up against the Caprock," Robinson said to Walk, "but that Indian girl says she knows a way down. She claims there is an alternate trail of the old comancheros that goes down the Caprock about here."

Walk looked at him. "What have you got to lose?" he asked grimly. "Your horses couldn't run much farther even if there was any place to run to. You better follow her."

"She's looking for it now."

Clay Hamilton had dismounted and was leading his limping horse. Walk went forward to the rim of the Caprock. It looked like an abyss, with the gray clouds rolling and settling, showing nothing but vertical walls that went down out of sight. Somebody shouted to Robinson above the crackle of the fire. "She found it!"

Men began disappearing over the edge. Robinson shouted orders at the rear guard, and they began to pull back. Men, horses, and mules went down into the rolling gray clouds and out of sight.

Walk waited with Robinson. "What happened to Gault?" the lieutenant asked Walk.

Estacado spoke up from behind them in his Arkansas drawl. "He ran into the wrong end of a grubbing hoe," he answered.

The heat from the advancing fire was strong on their skin before every man was down. One mule balked.

"Shoot it!" Robinson ordered.

"It isn't necessary," said Walk. "Mules are no good to Indians. Let it go. We may find it later."

An hour later all of them were at the bottom of the Yellowhouse canyon. Clay Hamilton figured they were two or three miles from his ranch house. The cavalry troop reformed, and the wounded got attention by the light of a small brush fire. They had left one dead man up on the prairie—the flank guard who had been killed in the initial attack.

The ranchmen began to strike out for their homes under clouds of smoke that made a low, dense-black ceiling. The smell of burned grass was strong and now there was the pungent aroma of bruised sage. Downcanyon a cow bawled, nervous from the reflection of fire in the sky and the echoing shouts of men at night. Madeline, Walk, Quita, and Estacado rode single file across the sagebrush, with Madeline leading the way. Clay Hamilton had gone ahead with the ranchmen.

Walk, riding behind Madeline, said, "I figger the fire will burn itself out against the Caprock by tomorrow night."

Madeline's voice came back to him as the blue roan picked his way among the mesquite bushes in the dark. "There'll be a lot of good grass destroyed."

"There's lots more," said Walk. "The Plains reach halfway across New Mexico."

"Are you going back to trade with the Indians?" she asked after a moment.

Walk said judiciously: "I reckon not. Things are liable to be pretty warm on the Plains for a while. Gault is gone, but the Indians are already stirred up. There'll be trouble."

"Maybe you'll go next year," she suggested. They

216

were out of sight of the cavalry fire by now.

"No, ma'am, I don't think so. The comanchero trade won't last long anyway. This outbreak tonight will bring the Army back, and I reckon the Indians will be cleared off the Plains in another year. And that's the end of the comanchero. In fact, I figure tonight is the end, for the Indians won't be doing much trading while the Army is after them."

"You lost everything but your stock," she said.

Walk was grimly amused. "Well," he said, "I gambled. I came out here to pick up a ranch quick, and for little or nothing. I reckon I haven't any squawk coming." He watched the sorrel's white mane lift and fall as she picked her way, following the blue roan. "I've still got 2,500 silver pesos up there in what's left of an Army wagon. That was in custody of the Army, and I can get it back."

"The Indians will take it."

"I doubt the Indians will investigate the burned-up Army wagons before tomorrow morning, and by that time they'll be scattering, because they know the Army will come back. Anyway, Indians don't have much use for money—never did." They rode in silence for a moment. "How'd you like to go in partnership with me?" Walk asked.

"Partnership?" she echoed.

"Sure. Maybe I can get some work down here in the canyon and look for Lost Spring on the side. When I find it, we can start a ranch up there and raise cattle— and cowhands, maybe." He was glad it was dark. His face was hot.

There was silence up ahead, broken only by the sound of Walk's gloves slapping against the cantle. Then Madeline's clear voice came back, "I've been

217

investigating that Lost Spring legend for years, and I'm satisfied it's just talk." She paused. "But I know something that beats it."

"What's that?" he asked, thinking she had missed the implication of his statement, and beginning to recover from his embarrassment, a little disappointed, but also a little relieved.

"Shorty and I used to go up there to look for stock. We were resting one day, and Shorty got to arguing about how deep a prairie-dog hole was. I bet him a dollar it wasn't over four feet deep, so we pitched in and dug one out." She paused.

Estacado's voice came up from behind Walk somewhere. "That's why them strange piles of dirt was up on the Plains." His voice lowered. "How deep was it, ma'am?"

"Twelve feet," she said, and added, "and it was just above water. If you dig down twelve or fifteen feet, you can find water some places up there."

Walk asked in amazement, "Is that a fact?"

"That's a real fact," she assured him. "Shorty and I never told anybody, and I imagine land up there could be bought for about five cents an acre right now from the State of Texas. But," she went on, "it may be, as you said, some time before it's safe." She paused and seemed to draw in a deep breath. "In the meantime," she went on, a little faster than she usually talked, "my father holds some mortgages on Gault's outfit. Why don't you buy in? We might as well go into partnership and start raising ranch hands in the valley."

Walk gulped. There was dead silence except for the cracking of brush under the horses' hoofs and the slapping of his gloves against the saddle. He was thankful for the dark. His face was burning, and he

218

knew from Madeline's last rush of words that hers must be too.

Then her voice came again, low and hesitant. The blue roan had slowed down and was barely ahead of the sorrel, and he could see Madeline's outline, small but sitting straight in the saddle. "There's one thing bothering me, Walk. What would you do about Quita?"

Walk swallowed. "I want you to know I traded Flying Bear out of the blue roan with the idea of giving him back to you—but you see—" He paused, not knowing quite how to say it.

Quita's cheerful voice floated out of the darkness behind him. "I tell truth about Señor Andale buying me with the horse to keep Ramón from whipping me, and I tell truth that he tried to send me home—if you let me work for you. Is hard work—raising *niñas*," she said.

Estacado smacked his lips somewhere behind Quita. "That there sounds like a good deal to me," he said. "That little squaw can make the best prairie-dog soup you ever set your teeth in."

"I take care of fire too," she said. "You cut firewood. Andale and the *señora* can ride around digging up prairie-dog holes, while I catch dogs and make soup. O.K., Chief?"

Walk pushed the sorrel alongside the blue roan. Estacado's nasal drawl floated out of the darkness behind. "I don't reckon she's takin' the place of a man now," he said.

No one answered, but presently Walk's voice came low: "Answerin' your question, ma'am—because I figger when a lady asks a man a question she's entitled to an answer—answerin' your question, I can't see any good reason why we can't do just exactly what you suggested."

219

There was silence again. Quita and Estacado stopped their horses, for up ahead the blue roan and the sorrel were no longer moving, and there was not even the sound of Walk's gloves slapping against the cantle.

We hope that you enjoyed reading this
Sagebrush Large Print Western.
If you would like to read more Sagebrush titles,
ask your librarian or contact the Publishers:

United States and Canada

Thomas T. Beeler, *Publisher*
Post Office Box 659
Hampton Falls, New Hampshire 03844-0659
(800) 818-7574

United Kingdom, Eire, and
the Republic of South Africa

Isis Publishing Ltd
7 Centremead
Osney Mead
Oxford OX2 0ES England
(01865) 250333

Australia and New Zealand

Bolinda Publishing Pty. Ltd.
17 Mohr Street
Tullamarine, 3043, Victoria, Australia
(016103) 9338 0666